# OFF
# MY
# FEET

# OFF MY FEET

*a novel*

*rachel tremblay*

Copyright © 2020 Rachel Tremblay

All Rights Reserved

ISBN: 978-0-9690172-7-1

E-BOOK: 978-0-9690172-9-5

*GrindSpark Press*

GrindSpark
Press

*www.rachel-tremblay.com*

*f*

*o*

*r*

*m*

*i*

*t*

*c*

*h*

We are stardust. Highly complex puzzles made of the myriad pieces of carbon let loose from the explosion of a gazillion-year-old ball of glowing, hot gas. That's us. All we are is intelligent dirt. I know this, and still every day I rise to the rays of the sun, a different sun than the one that made us, but a warm and galvanizing one nonetheless. Every day, I rise refreshed. That is, until I remember my life. Until I go to work. Then, all I am is bored. And that's a safe and comfortable way to be. There are no sharp corners in my world. Plus, there's free coffee. And you can't really complain about much when you have free coffee. So that's who I am. I am Edie. I am sun-loving dirt, and I like coffee.

# ONE

It's quiet. Radio music drives me nuts, so the hum of the fridge is the only sound travelling the room. The continuous purr is lulling, and it's a good thing I've got cup after cup of joe to keep me awake. Gut rut is inevitable, but then I'm so quickly bored again that it's worth it. This coffee buzz is the most interesting thing that'll happen to me today. I make myself another.

There aren't many customers; there never are. And those I get are rude, as usual. From a bird's-eye view, they all look the same. You could mash all my regulars into one big, rude-ass customer. The result: a medium-brown-haired, medium-height, chubby she-man that tips next to nothing, barks orders, and avoids eye contact. That last one kills me. All the humanity of an exchange leaves when eyes don't meet. Today I served such a regular. He always throws his loose change on the counter, talks on his phone, and avoids looking at me in the face. I refer to him as Jack. Jack Ass. Jack is almost the perfect chubby she-man blend of all rudeness. Except that Jack tips big. I guess he thinks money makes up for his lack of humanity. I don't.

I'm always broke, but I have a lot of humanity. I think. I look people in the eye all the fucking time.

"Hi there," I say to a lady walking in, looking her right in the face. See? But she's uncomfortable and looks away. It doesn't surprise me. Maybe I come on too strong. I tend to think that because I serve them, the invisible wall that usually keeps people from speaking to one another is automatically knocked down. But I often find myself just speaking through that wall, through the people, right through the door. Maybe I'm actually talking to some kid walking down the sidewalk, cone in his hand and ice cream dripping over his knuckles. He's not listening either. He's focussed on licking himself clean. It's always the same. Everyone is focussed on their own shit. And really that's just fine. It's not as if I want them all up in my bubble anyway. The lady takes her coffee and chooses a seat by the window.

I wipe down some tables and thread my fingers through the handles of a few stranded cups. I can easily carry eight or ten this way, but I rarely have the chance. My shop, *Café L'Aimé*, is always empty. People mostly take their coffee to go. I wipe down the tables for the umpteenth time today. They're so damn clean I can see myself in them, even though their glass tops are all scratched up. I look down in one and fix my medium-brown, medium-length hair. It's tucked in a low bun, and there's not much to fix.

The weather's great, so I step out with my cold, damp rag, plant my fists on my hips and stand for a while in the warm, blazing sun. Why that lady is sitting inside, I don't know. She's probably afraid someone will walk by and look her in the face.

There are only two tables out here, and if anyone happens to come by the shop and stay, this is usually where they sit. I don't blame them. They have the best view: across the street is the Spin Factory, and through those front doors is a world of music to discover. Well, the view doesn't have much to offer, because I can never see inside from here. Not that I try to.

The windows look black thanks to the bright sun, and even though I squint, I can't see inside at all. It doesn't matter. I'll go at lunch time, as I do every day, and flip through the vinyl records. I'll choose one at random, place it on one of the turntables, put on the headphones, and, with utmost loving care, drop the needle. For a short half hour, as I switch from one record to the other, my boring-ass life will be sweet.

I lied. This is the most interesting part of my day.

I nod to the guy at the cash register. He nods back and continues with his transaction. Someone is buying a Blue Note record. I recognize the royal-blue stripes. I get a good feeling from watching people buying quality records. I know they'll go home and put it on, first thing. Maybe they'll pour themselves a drink, dim the lights, strike a match, light a candle, and then a cigarette with the same flame. They'll lick the tips of their fingers and put out the match, place it gently on the candle's dish, sit back and put their feet up. They'll take a puff, exhale, and listen.

That never happens to me, because I never buy anything good.

The random music of choice today is Frank Zappa and the Mothers of Invention, Nana Mouskouri, and A Tribe Called Quest. Each in their turn, they ease the suffocating awareness of impending death; the end that awaits us all. For a while, my mundane life is transformed into something much more interesting, where the ticking of invisible clocks doesn't loom behind my thoughts, reminding me constantly that this is it. I'm thirty years old and this is my life.

My lunch break is over, so I grab another Phil Collins from the one-dollar bargain bin. Just an excuse to show that I'm a paying customer.

"I don't think I have this one," I say to the guy, ashamed of how many Phil Collins albums I have. I give him the buck and head out.

On the way home, I cross a beggar and his red kiddie wagon full of plastic bags. Every day he parks there, in front of the liquor store. His name is Frank. It suits him well. He is the most honest and rude person I know. Worse than any of my customers, even Jack.

I drop a quarter in his paper plate.

"You're a cheap bitch!" He looks up at me with bloodshot eyes. A waft of nasty beer breath floats up to my nose.

"I know, Frank. But hey, don't spend it all in one place." I tap his shoulder a couple of times, a cloud of filth puffing up from his dirty jacket.

A bit further is a plant shop, and Jane is feeding those hanging outside. The whole storefront is framed in green, the doors behind them a dark entrance into an intriguing jungle.

"Hey, Edie, I have another one for you. A baby fern."

"Thanks, Jane."

She hands me the plant grown from offcuts and broken shoots. A smile, and her attention is back to the watering can. She never expects money. I don't know why she does it. It must have been tiring to watch me admire her plants, day after day, without ever buying any. Jane has been contributing to my personal jungle for years, and if she expected payback, I'd owe her quite a bit by now.

Feeling indebted is the worst. But what I hate even more is when a person does something nice, for no reason, and then expects something in return. Of course, they won't tell you; it's an unspoken understanding. But the weight is palpably there, hanging over your head every time you meet, and the guilt doesn't go away until you either reciprocate, or start avoiding them. Be too generous with a person and surely you will push them away. Even if no one likes to, it's natural to feel indebted to kindness. People are rarely nice for no reason.

I don't think Jane expects anything, because there's never any weight to her donations. That's the only reason I accept them.

The walk home takes a total of forty minutes, give or take, including the shoulder taps and plant adoptions. Most of it is spent on a sidewalk that hugs banks, government buildings, restaurants, and parks. It's usually refreshing; the kind of refreshing that involves seeing lots of interesting people doing much more interesting things than I'll ever do. Like riding motorized scooters, picnicking on a blanket with friends, or wearing fancy, new clothes. Well, either it's refreshing or depressing. Probably both.

There's no rumble, but the sky is a solid white, and rain starts to drop. So today I guess it's refreshing for everyone. By the time I get to the small grocery store kitty-corner to my place, my shoes are soaking wet. It makes no difference that they have holes in the heels; I'm soaking wet all over. So is baby fern, but he doesn't mind.

My bank account says fifteen dollars; I check on my smartphone under the awning before going in. So rice and beans it is. I grab a few ingredients and look the cashier right in the eyes as I pay for them.

Sitting near the door of my building is a black-and-white tabby, its fat bottom melting into the concrete. It must squat nearby, because it waits for me every day.

"It's raining. What are you doing, crazy cat?" Its ears are flat on its head, clumps of fur pointing in all directions. His face fur is long, resembling a moustache and beard, his wonky coat spotted and striped, not typical of a tabby cat, but the "M" on its forehead clearly drawn. It looks up at me with a face both expectant and grumpy, knowing I have jerky in my pocket. I crouch down. As soon as the meat is secured between its teeth, it takes off. Only once in the many years I've lived here have I succeeded in petting it.

The door to my apartment building opens up to two more doors behind it. The left one leads to my flat, upstairs, and on the right is my neighbour's. James is his name, and he is standing in the entrance behind the first door when I step in.

"Hello, Edie."

"James."

"I got your mail here, Edie. It's your lucky day. You have a package. The mailman wasn't going to leave it with me, but I convinced him. Told him we were close friends." He puts the package in my outstretched hand.

James and I are not close friends at all. I can tell he wants something from me. Probably sex. Or worse: a relationship. He's that kind of guy. I hate it when he does nice things for me. His favours, unlike Jane's, come with incredible weight. And I don't want any of it. So I don't thank him, because that would encourage him, but I still look him in the face, because that's what I do. An annoyed sigh is all I give, and hopefully that's enough to let him know what I think. That James, I don't trust him one bit. As I said, people are rarely nice for no reason.

The package tucked under my arm, bags hanging from my wrists, and plant in hand, I manage to unlock my door. It slams on its loose hinges, right in James's face. I don't feel bad.

The light is still bright in my apartment. That's one of the best things about summer when you live far from the equator. The sun sets late and the days feel much longer. The coffee shop closes at six every night and that gives me a few daytime hours to do what I please. But it makes no difference. My life is boring as hell.

Dozens and dozens of plants on the floor, windowsills, corners and ledges; nooks filled with cheap keepsakes and vintage knick-knacks. I'm a sucker for a deal. That's all I can afford anyway. But I have taste and my junk is gold. I put baby fern and the groceries on the counter and plop off my ratty shoes. My apartment isn't all that great, but I've been here a long time so my rent is cheap. With roommates it'd be even cheaper, but you need friends for that. Anyway, think of all the crap those friends would bring in and spread, certainly in the most careless fashion, all over my apartment. And all the chatter that would be going on, all the time. The parties they would throw. No, alone is better. So what if I'm broke? There's not much I need. Sometimes I dream of owning a TV, but most times I don't mind.

I pull Phil Collins out of my tote bag, wipe away a few raindrops that got through, and place him close to where his twins are stashed. I flop onto my couch with the package and turn it around in my hands a few times. Brown wrapping. I rip it open. It's replacement parts for my coffee machine, ordered for me by my sister. To buy things online you need a credit card, which I don't have. Even though I don't like owing money, not to anyone—

and Emily is no exception—my machine will be working again. And that's just more important.

Plastic milk crates line the wall, possibly where a TV would be set up, and in them are my shitty records. At work, the radio stays off because my vinyl bins are full of the same crap. There's only so much one can take. I finger through rough cardboard edges thoughtfully, though it hardly makes a difference; it's all seventies or eighties pop, and some weird foreign stuff, and I'm mostly sick of it all. Phil is on the ground leaning against a red crate. I decide to do what the fancy people and their Blue Note records fresh from the store do, and pop it on right away. It cost me 99c and I dance for free, in my barebones living room, soaking wet and almost happy.

# TWO

Work is the same as every other day. Jack is back. I bend my knees real low and slant my head so that he might be forced to look at me, even if accidentally. He doesn't. I could act up. I could start singing, do jumping jacks while he gives me his order, stomp loudly and throw straws left and right while blowing raspberries. I could squirt him with caramel syrup. Instead, I overpack his espresso and scald his milk.

"Here's your karma, I mean latté," I say.

The sandwich I brought for lunch is wolfed down. It tastes so much like it does every other day that it basically tastes like nothing. I grab a to-go and lock the door behind me after flipping the sign that says "back in half an hour". Truly, a delicious part of my day. Flip. I jaywalk to the Spin Factory for my daily dose of melodies.

A few people are perusing the aisles. One is at a listening station going through a stack of potentials. The electronica section is empty, so I gravitate there.

From the corner of my eye I see someone walking straight towards me. It's the guy who works here. He's smiling at me from the other side of the waist-high row I'm flipping through. Why is he smiling at me? I wipe the milk moustache I imagine to be on my face.

"Hi," he says.

I twirl, expecting to see toilet paper trailing behind me.

"I found a real gem in the bargain bin I thought you might enjoy. I've put it aside for you," he says.

All these years, and this is the first time he suggests something to me. Am I blushing? Certainly not. He goes back to the counter and returns with a brightly coloured record sleeve.

"Give me that," I say, snatching it away, and walk over to a turntable. I slip on the headphones. It's really good. It's like jazz meets pop meets garbage.

"It's Japanese," he says, standing beside me, but I don't hear him because I have headphones on. I slip off an ear.

"It's Japanese," he says again.

"I love it," I tell him. But I show no emotion. I don't know what he wants from me, and I don't want to encourage his kindness before I know his intentions. What if he wants to slowly swindle me into buying expensive records? He knows I don't spend more than 99c at a time. I slip the record back into its sleeve, place the dollar in his hand and hop back over to my shop with the Japanese band in my bag.

On the walk home, I give Frank his quarter, he calls me a cheap bitch, and I nod at Jane. No plant today. I hear a flap flap noise and look around. It's one of my shoes. The heel has come undone. I wonder what the hell I'm doing with my life.

Morning come, the sun pours in through my unobstructed windows. As much as I love coffee, the sun has an even greater effect on me, waking me up better than three shots of espresso. The open curtains let the glow of the lampposts seep in at night, but it doesn't affect me; I always sleep like a baby. And I never have nightmares, though I rarely remember my dreams. It's just as well. Sleep is my blissful oblivion, somewhere to leave everything behind and lose myself in well-being and well-being alone. I need my sleep. I rely on it, I love it most dearly, and you best not fuck with it.

It's Tuesday—my only day off, scheduled specifically to coincide with card-playing day at the Cedar Residence, a home for the elderly. Old folks are great. Sure they bitch and whine a lot, and give way too much unsolicited advice, but they're honest, and they don't really give a hoot what you think of them. Best of all, they're not out to gain anything off you. They mostly just enjoy the company.

"Hi, it's me," I say into the intercom at my sister's building. She lives across town, and the Cedar Residence is a ten minute walk from her place. It takes two bus rides to get here, so I only come once a week. It was Emily's idea that I volunteer some time, after she heard me express fondness for the older generation. We rarely spoke (we still don't, and she knows little more about my life now than she did then), yet it wasn't hard for her to piece together that I spent most of my free time alone. I didn't hate the suggestion, so I decided to give it a shot.

Plus I knew it made her happy to see me, even if it was just a flyby. That was a year ago. With Fritz by my side, we haven't missed a card day since.

A few moments later I see her through the door's window. A tall brunette, sophisticated, even in her jogging pants. I've always felt clunky compared to her. I'm just not as slender or graceful. Our heights are similar, but I've got more muscle, and would be picked first on any schoolyard team. You almost wouldn't think we were sisters. That's because we're not. Emily was adopted. Not that it changes anything.

A furry face pokes its nose through the open crack of the door and squeezes through, too impatient for it to widen. Fritz jumps and puts his paws on my thighs, much to my sister's disapproval. Fritz is a well-behaved dog. He doesn't break his dog-rules with anyone but me. At the old folks' home, he is a perfect gentleman.

Curly balls of white hair are scattered around the common room. At the back, one person sits on a couch facing a wall-mounted TV. Her head bobs as she watches a ballroom-dance competition, the contestants wearing big numbers on their outfits and airbrushed smiles on their faces. The volume is too low to distinguish a melody but there's just enough rhythm coming through to permit this granny's grooving. She must have a pretty decent hearing aid, I think to myself. Another man sits alone, rubbing his wrinkly hands together, his thoughts zeroed in on the floor. His name is Mac. It makes me sad to see him always by himself, off to the side. He doesn't like to be touched. So I just say, "Hi, Mac." His eyes flick up, staring for three Mississippis, before landing back on the floor. I wonder what he's thinking about. Another person knits what seems to be a long scarf. Her fingers work fast, her needles clickety-clacking like tap shoes. She looks up and smiles. A more substantial cloud of salt-coloured hair is clustered around a circular table in the centre. Fritz runs up to it, too quiet to disrupt the conversation.

"George? No, he's still alive. He visited you yesterday!" one old man yells, his wrinkled lips curling over his gums where his teeth should be. He turns and mutters under his breath, "You can't even remember yesterday? You dumb kook."

"I heard that!" yells another impossibly old man. His cheeks sag past his jaw bone and dangle like turkey wattles.

"What about Janet? She's been sick for so long," says an old woman in a bright-green dress, her eyes shining black dots squeezed between folds of reddish eyelids.

"Oh, she died just last Tuesday," says another lady in a sweet, high-pitched voice. "So sad. Her whole family was here. Didn't you hear them? They were so noisy."

"Noisy kooks," mutters the first old man.

"Is Mick Jagger still alive?" asks the woman in the green dress. She smiles dreamily as she remembers something.

"I'm not sure," answers her lady friend.

"Mick Jagger. Now there's a kook!"

Fritz, sitting at the feet of one of the ladies, cuts in with a whimper. He's soon invited onto her lap.

"Hello, dear," she says, turning towards me. That's Olive. She used to walk to school in snowshoes, as a child. She tells me every time I visit. "You're just in time. Come sit right here." She pats the empty chair beside her.

We play a game of gin rummy and take turns commenting on either how long it takes a person to play his turn or how sunny it is outside. The common room is well lit thanks to the large east-facing windows. I don't know if all homes for the elderly are this cheery, but big windows and morning sun will make a difference in just about anyone's life. Even Mac's, I'm sure. I look over to the person watching the TV, who's missing out on the sunshine and the card game. Her head lolls over. She looks dead. I hope she isn't.

After the game, we sing. "What a Wonderful World" by Louis Armstrong, "That's Amore" by Dean Martin, and "As Time Goes By" from the movie Casablanca; the usual. A few harmonies are crooned in shaky voices, and I'm reminded once again why old folks are so damn awesome.

I accompany Olive back to her room. She takes baby steps with her walker and refuses all help.

"It's my workout," she tells me. Fifteen minutes to go down the hall, up an elevator, and back up the hall until we get to number forty-five. That's where Olive lives, and where I spend my Tuesdays combing her hair after the card games and songs.

"So, have you found a man yet, Edie?" Olive says in her small, jittery voice, laying her hands in her lap, ready for the gossip. Old people love to hear about your love life.

"No, Olive, not yet."

"You need to get married, Edie. You're not getting any younger, you know. You need to get out there and *meet* people."

I chuckle and continue to braid her long, grey strands, sitting cross-legged behind her on the bed.

"Once you've married, your life will be full," she continues. "You won't need to come here on Tuesdays anymore."

"I like coming here on Tuesdays."

"I like that you do, too, but ..."

"I don't like people, Olive."

Olive tries to turn her head to look at me over her shoulder.

"Are you a lesbian?"

"No, I just don't like people, in general. They're mean and untrustworthy. I'm happy on my own."

Fritz is snuggled up against her thigh on the edge of the bed. She strokes him, turning her gaze to the trees outside her window. I get back to the braid, and Olive continues to try to convince me of the benefits of marriage.

"You'll be sad without a man, Edie. You know, my life changed when I married Albert. For the better. He was liberal, mind you, and let me do as I pleased, unlike some ladies I knew who couldn't even go to the cinema without an escort."

"You're so wild, Olive," I say, finishing her hairdo and smoothing it all down once more with my hands.

"I know!" She giggles.

I return Fritz to my sister's and hop onto the next bus. My thoughts are on Olive. That she thinks I need a man doesn't bother me. What does is knowing that she doesn't have forever to live. She tells me she's quite ready to move on to the next adventure. That's something I'm not quite ready to think about. Olive has been more of a family to me in this short spin around the sun than I've ever had, even when my mother was alive. So, I would prefer Olive to stick around for a while yet.

The second bus usually drops me right on my street corner, but the street has been blocked off. There are police cars and fire trucks and a great amount of smoke. Huge billows, in fact, filling the sky. The driver opens the door and lets me off as close as he can. He doesn't look me in the face as he usually does; he's focused on the chaos outside. One loss for humanity, one win for chaos.

The sidewalk is crowded with rubberneckers. I push my way to the yellow tape, a policeman stopping me just as I duck to pass under it.

"There's no passing, Miss."

"But I live right over there," I say, just as I realize it's my apartment building that is burning. Flames raging through my gorgeous, light-welcoming windows, licking up the brick siding and blowing out puffs of cremated tables, plants, knick-knacks and couches. My golden junk is burning.

"Nooo!" I yell.

"Miss, you have to back up."

"But that's my home!"

The policeman leans into his chest pocket where his walkie-talkie is tucked in and speaks some unintelligible crap into it. Soon another policeman arrives and the first one points to me.

"That one," he says.

"You can come with me," the second one says, leading me through and across the street to his vehicle.

James is sitting sideways in the back of the cop car, his legs hanging out the open door. He has a blanket on his shoulders and his cheeks glisten with tears.

"Edie!"

"Hey, James." I feel like I should say something comforting to him. He seems to be taking it much harder than I am, and wonder then if I, too, should be crying. "Well, this blows, huh?"

"Blows? This is devastating! My collections!" He starts sobbing again. James collects a variety of things. Nothing cool like books or paintings or creepy dolls; nor weird curiosities like belly button lint or something equally disgusting. No, he collects snow globes and decorative spoons. That kind of stuff. He has more salt-and-pepper shaker sets than any one person should ever own.

"Mickey and Minnie," I remind him. And a fresh wave of tears burst from his red face.

I lean on the car beside him and watch the firemen from afar, shooting tons upon tons of water into the window holes. Seeing James cry over his salt shakers is sobering. It's just stuff. I'm glad we will only collect insurance money and not barbecued pets. Still, my heart squeezes for my dozens and dozens of plants, my shitty vinyl collection, and my freshly fixed coffee machine.

# THREE

It's 7 p.m. by the time they put the fire out. People are circulating again, their conversation energized with excitement, their eyes sparkling. Easy when it's not your place that burnt down. My phone has two bars of juice. I find my insurance company on the internet and get hold of an agent through an emergency number. He shows me as much empathy as a cryogenically frozen ex-boyfriend. Not that I'm calling for moral support. But I do need money and a place to stay. My sister would help, I'm sure, but I've no desire to call her, and no one else to call but her. So I turn to "the man", who directs me to the Bednest Inn. My policy will cover my hotel stay for up to two weeks. As far as money goes, I can come in to the office tomorrow and collect a small courtesy cheque.

Typing in my information, the desk clerk at the Bednest Inn screws his face into his computer. James, having just checked in, waits beside me.

"Staying at the same hotel is great," he says. "We can be there for each other. You know, these are hard times. We could save money by staying in the same room, too. It would be a smart thing to do. I know your insurance is paying for your room, but I'm fronting mine, so it's dinging my wallet more than yours. I'm fine, though. I mean, I've got money. And I like to spend money, but saving is good. I could stay in your room. Or, you could stay in mine, you know. I don't mind paying. Save your insurance some money. I could sleep on the couch. I don't know if there's a couch, but I could sleep there. Or, on the floor, even. Though that's a bit sad, don't you think? If we get a double bed, we could share. That's not a problem. I know how to keep my hands to myself…"

I tune him out, keeping my eyes on the clerk, who is searching for an east-facing room as he strokes a calico cat on his lap with his free hand. Realizing the futility of his efforts, James leaves, dragging his feet all the way to the elevator.

"There are no east-facing rooms left, Miss Stacks," the clerk says. "Actually, that man there took the last one."

"Him?" I point to James, who has just pressed the elevator button. The clerk nods and I show him my index, requesting a short moment.

"James." I tap him on the shoulder just as the elevator doors open. He turns, his spirits suddenly uplifted. "James, they have no more east-facing rooms. I need an east-facing room. You need to trade with me."

"I don't *need* to do anything," he answers, a smile growing as he realizes the bargaining chip he now has. Knowing my habits isn't necessary; he can tell by my eager tone, which I never use with him.

"Just stay with me," he says.

"No, James."

"Well, then, what are you willing to trade for it?"

"Trade? I don't know. I can find you really cool salt-and-pepper shakers, to start your collection again. I have a knack for finding ..."

"A date."

"What?"

"I'll give you the room if you go on a date with me," he says.

I chuckle. "James, please, the room."

"You heard me."

I suddenly picture myself sitting at a table across from him, a fake laugh erupting from my lips as the waiter pours us more champagne, my black dress sparkling with sequins, his bow tie so tight his face glows bright red, his eyes bulging as he holds up a salt shaker for me to see.

"Never mind. Keep the room."

I walk back to the counter.

"Give me what you got," I say to the clerk, and collect the keys.

He turns back to his computer, petting the purring critter as he scrolls.

"May I pet him?" I ask.

The clerk nods. The cat meets my hand halfway, obviously loving the affection, and I feel vindicated for every time I tried to pet my stray tabby. I wonder what'll happen to him. Maybe he'll lose a few pounds.

Only once James disappears into the elevator do I make my own way up.


It was an uncomfortable night, and a crappy morning. The strident beeping of my phone wakes me like sandpaper across my face, an ugly room dusted with a dull light greeting me as I open my eyes. I know I'm awake but feel like I'm still asleep, so cloudy my brain feels. For a moment I forget why I'm in this caving bed, coming to life in the dimmest of rooms.

It comes back to me, just like anything you'd rather forget. Anything you'd want washed away with a fresh day. It always comes back, unheralded and sneaky as fuck. Maybe you spent your whole pay cheque at the casino, or you got drunk and had sex with your best friend. You lied, you cheated, you stole, you ate two whole boxes of chocolate-chip cookies. You wake up feeling like shit and it doesn't take long to remember why. Maybe that big fight comes back to mind, flooding your insides with anxiety and regret.

But sometimes it's not your doing. Sometimes, morning brings to light what you would push away forever if you could. That thing you wish was just a bad dream. That thing that feels too real to be real. Someone is sick, missing, incarcerated, dead.

This morning, I remember my flat burned down. There are worse things, sure, but aren't there always?

Images of the blazing building drift through my mind, the smell of smoke hitching a ride with them. It really happened. I know because I'm awake, and the waking mind knows what's real. But it still feels like a dream.

The shower does little to bring me to my full senses. A bad coffee from the hotel restaurant is the last failed attempt at a decent start to my day. I drink it quickly, standing by a window, because it tastes like crap, and crappy coffee just isn't worth sitting down for. My mind skims over my thoughts from a bird's-eye view, watching them crash like directionless bumper cars, absorbing very little of it. All the while, my eyes scan the room. I expect to see James at the breakfast buffet, or at a table, checking out the condiment jars, maybe inspecting an interesting menu holder, but I don't. In fact, I have a feeling I'll never cross paths with the old softie again.

Though I wouldn't need to rush back, my sense of responsibility as the only employee sends me off to work in yesterday's clothes. Besides, I need to stay busy if I want to keep my mind from unravelling. Too much dwelling on problems can kill. Drag a person down into an abyss of self-pity and anger. I'd be toast if I didn't go back to work today. Not that work is stimulating. But it's still better than doing nothing.

Right beside my shop, I see an apartment for rent: a red and white sign dangling from a porch, and on it a phone number in large black digits. It must have been vacated recently, or perhaps I simply hadn't noticed it. It's funny how we tend to only see what's pertinent to us. We can go about our whole existence ignorant of what's just beyond our peripheral view, just because our experience never forced us to look it in the face. We don't see it, just like we don't see each other. We live out our days in a narrow corridor decked with curated information, curated people, recycled knowledge and regurgitated opinions.

So this is how I see the "for rent" sign, suddenly important to me. It seems logical to check it out, which I do after my long and dull, but necessary, day of work. In my pocket is the courtesy cheque I picked up from the insurance office during my extended lunch break. My agent, quite pleased that I wouldn't be racking up a bill for them, didn't hesitate to give me the equivalent of the two-weeks hotel stay I was covered for, and a little more. I didn't argue.

I squeeze in through the door just as someone leaves and walk up to the third floor. Door number eight is ajar, so

I let myself in. The landlady, a short, round woman in a white shirt and long black tie—a lady you could easily imagine playing poker and smoking cigars with a bunch of men without feeling out of place—walks up to greet me.

"You must be Edie," she mumbles. I can almost see the cigar dangling from her mouth. We shake hands.

It's a big place for the price. A loft-style apartment on the third floor in a nine-apartment building. Ten-foot-high ceilings, mahogany moldings, hardwood floors. Fridge and stove included.

"I'll take it if you'll have me," I say.

The landlady gives me a hearty laugh, holds out her hand, and then slaps it into mine.

"You just leave the rent money in an envelope on your counter here. I'll come by to pick it up in two days," she says. "I have keys to all these apartments, so don't worry about being here. I'll let myself in. Just leave the envelope."

"Wow, you're so easy going," I say. "Is there not anyone else in line for it?"

"Nah. I just put the sign up this morning. You're the first one to visit. It's all yours."

In exchange for a minimal amount of information and a signature on the lease papers, I get a set of two keys. Their tops are both covered with a piece of green painter's tape, black numbers sharpied onto them. Eight was my door number; fifty-one was the building.

"I hope you're a hard sleeper," she says in a mumbled grunt.

"Why's that?" I ask.

"The neighbours."

"Oh. Is it really bad?"

"No. Just thought I'd mention it. But I'll let them know someone new is here. Maybe they'll play nice. Don't tear the place up." And she walks away with a waddle.

The evening is spent running up and down the aisles of my favourite thrift store, filling my cart with some bare necessities: a plate, a fork, a spoon, a knife, a frying pan. One can get singles of anything at a thrift store. I also need at least one change of clothes, soap, a towel, and shit like toilet paper. Most of my money is spent on a bed, which I buy new. It's not the best one out there, but it's the best I can afford without sapping me dry.

The stores close at nine and my bed gets to my place shortly after I do, around nine thirty. It's so big it hardly makes it through my door, which is sandwiched between two other apartments. I lead the delivery men to the far end of the loft to put the mattress down by the east-facing windows. As if it would belong anywhere else.

I finally hit the sheet (I have only the fitted one, the cleanest I could find) and I'm so tired I'm already anticipating drool leaking across my cheeks. Stripped down to my T-shirt and undies, I climb in under my thrift-store blanket that smells of harsh laundry soap, and set my alarm for six. It happens, from time to time, that I sleep through the sunrise on grey, rainy days. Those days tend to be grumpy ones.

Tonight, I let myself expect nothing less than a good night's sleep on this perfectly new bed. What better way to assuage the tragic blow of the conflagration of my life. I laugh at the thought. It's not that tragic. I had almost nothing.

And I begin again, with almost nothing. A new page has been turned, I tell myself. One that might be filled with a more interesting story. But who am I trying to fool, really? I lay my head on my second-hand pillow, too indifferent to hope for anything better than what I had.

And then it starts. Low and mellow at first, a rhythmic and continuous moaning. A woman, just on the other side of my north wall. My exhaustion suddenly leaving, my eyes open with the weird curiosity only those particular sounds can evoke. She gets louder, and louder. Then a male voice enters the mix, keeping to the rhythm. I prop myself up on my elbows and listen, imagining what they look like. Two big, overweight humans, a couple of skinny nerds, long-haired hippies? Who knows. One cannot tell by hearing them, obviously, but I imagine them all the same.

Finally I lay my head back down. I'm tired but I can't sleep. It's 11:45 p.m., and the moans, the whimpers, and the grunts continue until 1 a.m. They finally stop, and I think I'm going to be able to fall asleep, but they start again a half hour later, and go on until 3 a.m. The curiosity is well drummed out of my head by now. I don't care what they look like, what position they're in, what colour bed spread they have or what the rest of the apartment looks like. I just want them to get off each other.

I wake in the dark under the pillow I had uselessly used to keep the sex noises out, after a few measly hours of sleep, to the sound of my disgusting phone alarm.

Slowly, I get ready for work. I think of the stout landlady warning me about the noise and wonder if this is what I have to look forward to every night.

As I step out of my apartment, I see them. The humping neighbours. They look refreshed, in contrast to me with the dark rings under my eyes. As it turns out, they are two regular, good-looking people. The girl is my height, long dark hair, thin. The guy is a bit taller, kind of lanky but muscular. Scruffy beard, shaggy hair. Great, now I can imagine them better, I think with sarcasm. We nod at each other, and I let them go down the hallway first so I can see what they look like from behind. I don't know why I do. I really don't want to imagine them better. But I know I will.

# FOUR

Lunch break doesn't come fast enough.

"Hey," I say to the record store clerk as I walk in. He seems surprised that I'm speaking to him. "I'd like to buy a record today, something of better quality than my usual."

His eyebrows rise and he smiles, coming out from behind the counter where he had been messing around with the ancient-looking cash register.

"What's the occasion?" he asks.

I don't answer, and instead raise my own eyebrows.

"Too personal," he says. "Ok. Well, I know you prefer regular rock to progressive, and you have a penchant for the weird. Maybe we should look at something experimental, in the jazz, blues, or indie rock."

It's off-putting how well he knows my tastes. All he ever sees me buy comes out of the cheapo bin by the counter, which isn't much of an indicator. Then I remember the records I leave at the station every day, obeying the sign that says "Let Us Put The Plates Away". That's years of daily clues. I tsk myself for leaving such a part of me exposed.

I follow him down the aisles as he flips and chooses records from the racks, hmm-ing and aah-ing.

"Dude, just one record."

"Yes, but you're going to be doing your regular exploring anyway, right?"

I am, so I let him pluck out records. It's making him so damn happy. He places them beside a turntable and backs away, giving me space.

The pile on the left-hand side gets moved one by one to the right as I go through them. The prices surprise me; for the first time in forever I look at them with the intent to pay. Some are still way too expensive for what I'm willing to dish out. I end up choosing a Jane Jane Pollock LP, priced at fifteen dollars.

The clerk looks at me funny as we exchange money. I avoid his curious eyes easily enough.

Outside, I pull the record back out of my tote bag and look at it some more. The door chime jingles, and the clerk steps out.

"Oh, hi again," he says.

He smiles and pulls out a cigarette.

"You smoke?" I then say, surprising myself with my nosiness. "That is so dumb." I remember my Blue Note fantasy involving candles and cigarettes and feel a tad jealous of his idiocy.

"Sorry to disappoint you."

He lights it and takes a drag, exaggerating his satisfaction as he exhales. I put the record back in the bag.

"What's your name, anyway?" he asks.

"What's *your* name?" I ask back. You'd think that the years of polite nodding would have been an indication of the level of privacy I enjoy. But no, he pries.

"Wolf."

"Of course you have the coolest name in existence." I'm feeling annoyed. "But I bet you got teased in grade school, huh? It was horrible, wasn't it?"

"I was homeschooled. My friends had names like Neptune and Vanilla."

"Boy. You guys would have been eaten alive. I was called *Eddie* until I had boobs. Not by choice, mind you. I mean, having boobs is great, it's just, my name's Edie. Grade school was a very confusing time."

Still holding the record, I carefully think about my next move. I put it back in the bag and extend my hand to the guy named Wolf. He shakes it.

"Very pleased to finally know your name, Edie with boobs."

"I gotta go back to work now," I say, taking my hand back. I give him a tiny smile before I cross the street and re-enter my cavern of dullness.

After work, I decide to walk out to Jane's shop even though it's not on my way anymore. Nothing's on my way anymore—I only need to take five steps to make it home. So I decide to detour my five steps into hundreds, because I want to pay for a plant. Jane's not there, and her replacement doesn't give a damn who I am. It makes sense, because it does not, in fact, matter who I am. I'm buying a three-dollar plant for god's sake. Go home, you pompous nut. I give Frank a dollar, and he still calls me cheap. But today he drops the "bitch". It's an improvement. I wonder how much it would take for him to say thanks.

The three-dollar plant looks good on the floor. My loft is still so bare, without a table, or a chair to tuck under it. For now I eat my veggies and hummus on my bed. I place the brand-new record down beside me, and remember that my turntable has been burnt to a crisp. My face flushes with heat and tears stream down my cheeks. While sadness or anger would have been justifiable, I know it's just fatigue.

"Get it together," I tell myself. I scramble to my purse, making the carrots fly, and fish out a pen and a coffee-stained envelope.

"Turntable," I mumble as I scribble it down. "Moooorrrre plaaants …" I pause there, thinking, and end up adding the few boring things that homes need to maintain a decent degree of cleanliness.

I keep busy doing some calisthenics and then shower. I hit the bed by ten, exhausted, only to be woken once more by the pleasure wails coming though the paper-thin walls. My eyes pop open and I stare at the ceiling, this time seeing their faces and mouths contort to match the sounds.

"You have got to be kidding me." I flip onto my side, laying my arm over my ear. Unhappy, but thinking it could always be worse, I close my eyes with an inkling of hope for sleep. Then a baby starts crying from behind the other wall.

I push myself to my feet and shuffle across the empty loft to the bathroom. On my way back I hear something else: a sewing machine, its sharp chugging coming up through the floorboards.

Indignant, I stomp back to bed and squeeze my head into my pillow like a taco. Despite my pessimism, it does all stop eventually. I check my phone, for the record. The glowing white numbers read 4 a.m.

Groggy and pissed. That's me. It's early morning, and, though I'm trustworthy with my boring-ass work, right now I only care about one shop. The pawn shop. I need to get my hands on a record player, and I'll feel panicked until I do. I'm not thinking completely straight, but there's nothing I can do about it, like I'm a kite caught in the wind, the end of my string snagging weakly through treetops.

I decide to flip the lunch-time window sign a few hours early and head out.

There are a couple of turntables to choose from. I get the cheapest and some equally cheap speakers. The insurance money hasn't come in yet, and though it's Friday and my measly pay cheque's been deposited into my account, I still have to restrain my spending. The courtesy money is almost gone, thanks to my new bed and the landlady's stealthy rent collecting, and that means if I buy this now, I'm dining on rice and beans all week. Hell, some things are just more important than food.

On my way back I cross a regular on the sidewalk.

"Where were you? I've been waiting for fifteen minutes!" she shouts.

"I'm sorry!" I yell back, my purchase under my arm and my step fast and heavy. A few more people are sitting at the tables outside, waiting.

"Sorry," I say again, and open the door for them. The turntable tucked behind the counter, I jump into a rush of grinding coffee, packing espresso, steaming milk, sprinkling cinnamon, all that crap. Everyone is just regular nice, regular rude. Everything is just regular, except that I'm sleeping at the wheel. Once they're all gone and the momentum is back to a standstill, gravity threatens to pull me down. I pour myself a filtered coffee before I fall on my face, and drag my body outside for some fresh air.

It's getting warmer out, the sun nearing its noon apex. It's going to be a nice one, and I won't be outside to enjoy it.

If I were a farmer, or a landscape artist, my days would be spent in the sun, in the dirt. That seems like a nice life. Or if I were a dog walker, or a park ranger. Or a bird. I could be a pigeon, and bob around in the park. Or the curb, pecking at crumbs in the cracks. I'd fly when I want to, hide when I want to, and just hang with other pigeons, or not, whenever the hell I feel like it.

Wolf comes out for a smoke. He stands in the shade of the awning and waves at me. He's a funny bird. Observant. More like a hawk, or a falcon. But not a pigeon.

He didn't puff on his poison out here before. Maybe he did out the back door, shamefully, like he should. No reason to share that with the world. Stupid cigarettes.

I watch Wolf bring his fingers to his mouth and imagine those are my lips, inhaling.

Come lunchtime, I'm where I always am, in his store. It's not his store, I don't think, just like my coffee shop isn't *my* coffee shop. Though, just like me, I think Wolf might be the only employee. I wonder if his boss is as non-existent as mine, leaving him on his own, day after day, serving others for measly pennies.

"Hi, Edie," Wolf says when I walk in. "Whoa."

"What?"

"Are you ok?"

"What do you mean?"

"You look like you lost a wrestling match with a mongoose."

"What the hell is a mongoose?" I straighten my hair a bit. I'm sure I brushed it this morning. My search through the racks is more uptight, my eyes looking up to see if Wolf is watching me and my mongoose-defeated face. I feel like this whole talking business might just be the ruin of the good thing we had going on. Which was no talking. I tsk myself again.

But he's not looking, so I listen to my records and let the rest melt into the decor.

The purchase of the day: a five-dollar Pavarotti and a thirty-dollar live Dizzy Gillespie. Screw the budget.

Two more plants are added to the sunlit floor. I lie down for a nap, that I might stay awake through some of the noise I suspect will plague the night, but I'm so overtired and so full of coffee that I can't fall asleep. I'm not much of a napper anyway. The ceiling stares back at me for ten minutes that feel like fifty before I decide to write in the notebook I bought myself. I'm documenting this shit.

That night I hit the sack a few hours earlier, and, as soon as the regular, good-looking people next door start doing each other, I get back up. My turntable ready, I pop on the Pavarotti record. Fight fire with fire.

The place sounds like a real zoo, if zoos caged opera singers, copulating humans, crying babies, nighttime seamstresses, and tap dancers. Yes, there was clear click-clacking coming from the apartment below me, beside the one with the sewing machine. And though less distinguishable, adding to the cacophony was a medley of sounds coming from first floor as well. It wouldn't have been much of a surprise to hear monkeys or see macaws fly by my window. No wonder the baby was crying.

Pavarotti howls, but the din still cuts through. I turn the volume up. Way up. Conducting an invisible orchestra with my only fork, it is in this way that I slip into the skin of the crazy fucker I'm becoming thanks to the night lunacy at building fifty-one.

# FIVE

Saturday is the busiest day at work. The shoppers, the sun soakers and city prowlers—they thirst for the life-giving drinks even more than the weekday folk, and they come through at all hours. It is a torturous morning, and I hate every second of it.

When lunchtime comes, I'm a pupil-less zombie. I sleepwalk across the street with my sandwich dangling from my mouth. Wolf almost chokes on his drink when he sees me.

"What the hell, Edie!"

"Huh?" I turn my head to him like a sloth towards a celery stick, or whatever. I'm so tired. He comes out to meet me and takes my elbows.

"Edie, what's going on?"

"Um." I wriggle out of his hold. "I haven't slept in three days."

"Why?" he asks as if it is a choice and I am an idiot.

"Becauuuse … my apartment burnt down last Tuesday. And now I live there." I point out the window at the building across the street beside the coffee shop. "And it's a zoo. A fucking *ZOO*, Wolf, if you must know."

"What are you talking about? Come, sit." He leads the way to a stool at the end of his counter. I sit.

"Well?"

"I can't sleep," I say. And then I start crying. I take a sharp sniff to catch the snot that threatens to leak down my lip, and wipe my eyes. "They're nuts. There's the baby. It cries, and cries, and cries; the tap dancer won't stop clacking, clackety clackety clackety … It's like firecrackers! And the sewing machines … How many people are fucking working down there? Huh? Is it a sweat shop? Is that why they do it at night? To hide it? I'm going to call Amnesty International. They'll put a stop to it. And they could stop the sex, too. So much sex. They're savages. All of them."

The hand patting my back would normally bother me, but I can't care.

"Have you tried earplugs?" Wolf asks.

"I did last night, after Pavarotti."

"Huh?"

"It didn't work. I'd have to line my walls and floors with carpet and egg cartons. I'm telling you, it's going to kill me."

"Damn. Let me think about this. Maybe I can be of assistance. Do you need any help getting through the afternoon?"

I shake my head, then lay it down over my folded arms on the edge of the counter and close my eyes.

That's how I get through the afternoon too. After each string of customers, I lay my head on my arms—these cushiony arms. Until the next one shows up. Jack, mister business-suit-too-good-for-you Jack, decides he's coming in on a weekend. Somebody hold me back. I'm going to kill him.

He tosses his coins on the counter, but I don't pick them up. Instead, I stare him down like a tigress. Or a really angry pigeon. He waits, talking on his phone in a low voice, but I don't budge. I am a wall, a mountain. And then it happens. His eyes look back at his money, they travel up to my torso, my neck … My heart rate rises; he's going to look me. Years, I've been waiting for this moment. Years! But just as he's about to reach my face, his eyes drop again, and he walks to the end of the counter to collect his drink. His half-allongé-half-americano-with-caramel-syrup bullshit drink. The only drink he ever orders. Of course, after the first two days of serving him, he never had to tell me his order again. People think they're so special when you know their special drink by heart. But there's nothing special about a bullshit drink. Black coffee. That's a special drink.

Cup in one hand and phone in the other, he leaves.

Fuck it. I put my head on the counter and wrap it tightly with my arms.

Under my ear is a magazine. The page bends, sticking to my face as I settle in to get comfy. Someone must have left it, right in my resting place. It smells strongly of perfume, like the fashion magazines you find in waiting rooms; the ones with the little tabs you have to lift and smell underneath, always fighting the urge to scratch it. Because you know it should be a scratch and sniff. Either way, they always stink, just like it stinks now. I don't care. I lie on the stinky magazine, lids drooping.

Large pink lettering catches my eye. Moving my arm but without raising my head, I read the words *sex noises*. Sleep-deprivation can really mess with your eyesight, apparently. Lifting off a few inches, I read again. "Sex noises keeping you up at night?" Well, now. This was written just for me. I stand straight and squint, forcing my brain to focus. Underneath the pink lettering reads: "All-natural sleeping pill, made from the exotic plant Tewtew, grown on the pacific island of Luumore. No side effects other than a good night's sleep."

My fingers suddenly too big for my phone, I attack it with clumsy taps.

"Emily," I say, panting.

"Edie, you sound panicked? What's going on?"

"No, it's fine. My flat burned down."

"WHAT?"

"It's ok. I already have a new place. But it's very, very noisy. And I haven't slept in days."

"That's horrible! Do you want to come sleep here?"

"No! No, that's fine. But I need to order this thing that'll help me sleep. So, I was wondering … could I use your credit card number? It's only twenty bucks. I'll pay you back."

God, I hate asking for help.

"You need more than that, Edie? It's not a problem."

"No, please." That's always my answer. *Please* instead of *thank you*. It's my way of asking that she doesn't insist.

She doesn't.

"Well, what kind of thing is this?"

"It's ... supplements. Helps your brain produce normal ... sleep stuff," I fib. Though I assume that's probably how it works. I have no idea.

There's a silence.

"Sure. D'you have a pen? I'll give you the number now."

I write it down, and am left with the dreaded feeling of indebtedness as we hang up. When the insurance money comes, and I hope it comes soon, I'll finally apply for a credit card. No more asking Emily.

My fat fingers go to work, poking the website address into my phone. The company is called *Cloud Nine Sleep*.

"Express shipping, please," I say to myself as I type in Emily's credit card number.

The afternoon finally ends. I'm starving, and remember the frozen burritos in my freezer. The thought helps me move forward. I lock the front door to the coffee shop after having done the worst clean up ever, and stumble over to the cursed fifty-one. I make it through the first doors, and absent-mindedly check my mail before heading up. There's a pink package stuffed in my mailbox. I pull it out. The return address reads "Cloud Nine Sleep", superimposed on a light-blue cloud. That is the fastest shipping I've ever seen. Though futile to think I'd remember to, I make a mental note to give them a good review.

The climb up to my apartment is painful. The next door couple is standing at their door, unlocking it, just as I turn into the hallway. They smile at me. I snarl. There's nothing that can alleviate my mood right now other than my burritos and a good night's sleep.

These pills take fifteen minutes to take effect. That's what's written in the short pamphlet enclosed in the pink envelope. I mow on my burritos while sitting on my bed and stare at the pictures of the *Tewtew* plant, a leafy, low-growing bush that apparently only grows in this one place on earth. A picture of workers standing in a field is printed on the back. They look happy. That's because they sleep well, of course.

I lick my fingers clean and crawl off my bed hands first, panda-rolling over to my small pile of clothes.

Sitting on the ground, I strip, struggle back to my feet, and do something I would never have dared to do before: flip the blinds. Next, I slip into bed.

My hand sweeps around me, feeling for the little pill jar. I reach for my glass of water on the floor. My hands are shaking, I'm so excited. The jar opens with a pleasing click. I put my nose to its edge—it smells like bubble gum. My fingers reach in, pull out a pink, oval pill, and place it on my tongue. I resist the temptation of sucking the taste off, because we all know it's bitter shit underneath a pill's coating. It goes down easily. After putting the jar and glass tumbler down, I lie on my back and place a rolled-up T-shirt across my eyes to block out any contemptible glimmer of light that might dare try to pry them open. Nothing is stopping me from going down tonight.

A few hours before the perfectly timed moans of the world's most well-pleased woman, I fall into a delicious sleep.

A yellow-brick road extends beneath my feet. On either side of the path is sky. I'm obviously dreaming. The road is lined with floating green bushes, bursting with colourful flowers. I pluck an orange explosion of petals and tuck it behind my ear. The sun is bright.

This is the best sleep ever, I think to myself. It's so quiet here. After a few tentative stomps on the levitating brickwork, I deem it safe and follow it down a small hill and into a wall of clouds. It's foggy and cool. I emerge on the other side at the entrance of a town road. Villagers stand outside their homes, as if awaiting me. I smile to them, and they wave back. Not creepy at all, I think to myself. This is a dream. The people are friendly. I can be friendly, too. So I wave my best royal wave as I walk through. Fireworks splatter the bright sky with colourful confetti and we all stop to ooh and aah. At the end of the road, a fat-bellied man invites me inside a tiny house. This somehow doesn't feel suspicious, and I bend down to follow him through the small door.

On the other side of this door is my coffee shop. The man walks to the counter and pulls a record out of a sleeve I don't recognize. The turntable I just bought is on the counter. He lays down the vinyl disk and places the needle on it. A fast, jazzy beat bursts through the speakers. I push the tables against the wall. The man asks for my hand, and we dance. Apparently I know the jitterbug. This is the best dream ever.

My alarm rings. It's dark under my T-shirt but I am almost ready to imitate my neighbours and moan with pleasure. Nothing beats a perfect night's sleep. Nothing.

I don't usually remember my dreams, but I recall last night's clearly, and it makes me smile. Looking up, I notice the sun trying to squeeze its fingers through the blinds, so I rush to the window to welcome it. Then I open the balcony door. Wind blows in, flinging my hair up like a bad shampoo commercial. Fragrance: Right As Fucking Rain. Below, the street is calm and empty, the treetops are green and happy, the birds are chirping. I look down at the Spin Factory and wonder which record I'll listen to today. It gives me the idea to put one on.

The Dizzy Gillespie in my hands, I swivel left and right. My record player is gone. I look everywhere: the closets, the cupboards, the bathtub, the garbage. Empty. I check my door for signs of breaking and entering. Nothing. But record players don't just vanish. Feeling disoriented, I decide to push my disappointment aside and figure it out later, because I really want to get back to my good mood. It's been so long. With a skip and a whistle, I get ready for work.

My face is almost normal. I practise a few smiles in the mirror.

"Not bad, not bad," I say, nodding. What a difference a good night's sleep can make.

My neighbours step out just as I do. I give them one of my practised mirror-smiles.

"Hello." The girl extends her hand. "My name is Eveleen, zis is Shaah-rl."

"Oh." I shake her hand, and then his. "Um, I'm Edie. Your neighbour."

"Yes," she says. "I am happy to finally spick. If we need a cup of ... sucre." She laughs.

"Sue-khr," I repeat.

"Euh, shoe-grrr," she says, giggling. I knew what she meant the first time. They walk away. "Bonne journée, Ee-dee!"

Though my inner pigeon protests, I make a conscious effort to be pleased with having made their acquaintance properly.

I unlock the coffee shop door and open it to find all the tables pushed up against the wall.

"What the hell," I mutter, guiding the door shut behind me. Was I here last night? I look over to the counter. My turntable is there, with the record still on it.

Going over the day before in my head, I clearly remember locking up and stumbling home, eating a badly thawed burrito, taking the pink pill and sleeping like a baby. And in my dream, I had danced, here, in my coffee shop. It was a dream. Had I sleepwalked with my record player? Where the hell does one get a jitterbug record in the middle of the night? Dazed, I pull the tables and chairs back out, set up my machines and start a few filtered coffee pots. I think of playing the record, but it creeps me out just enough to leave it. I decide to turn the radio on.

Customers come in and out. All is normal, except the bad music playing from the small corner speaker above the exit. A few regulars comment on it, pleased. The energy is a touch uplifted. You can always count on fluffy pop music to erase any deep thoughts. Somehow it doesn't bother me as it used to, instead bringing back happy memories of my bad record collection. It's the buoy that keeps me afloat this morning, making sure I don't sink into some dumbing confusion.

The best thing to do is just carry on as usual, I think to myself. What good would it do to sit and mull when there is no explanation I can come up with as to why the tables were all pushed aside this morning. Or how my turntable was brought down. Someone else might have an explanation. But not I. So I carry on.

# SIX

"Don't you eat lunch?" Wolf asks as he sees me walking in.

"Hi to you, too," I say, heading for the indie rock section.

"Hey," he calls out.

I stop before getting to my destination and turn towards him.

"You look a bit better," he says. "Have your neighbours taken a break from each other?"

"No. I'm taking supplements. It works."

"Supplements?"

I turn back around and continue. He catches up to me, stopping midway to pull out a record.

"I thought you'd enjoy this." He hands it over. It's Motown.

He's annoying me, but I go straight to the turntables to put it on. He follows and waits to see my reaction. Eyeing him on and off, trying to let him know he's cramping my style, I get distracted by the groove.

"Oh, shit."

"I knew you'd like it."

Our heads bob in sync. He can only hear what's leaking out of my headphones but he obviously knows what I'm hearing.

"Sold!" I say, realizing how loud I'm speaking when I make a few heads turn in the store.

The transaction is conducted in a careful way. I don't want to accidentally touch Wolf's hands. Now that we are on talking terms, I must be vigilant to not send him the wrong message. Sometimes you're nice to a guy, and he automatically thinks you want him. Or if they're nice to you, they expect your gratitude and friendship and who knows what in return. Need I repeat, people are rarely nice for no reason. I'd love to think otherwise, to have life prove me wrong. Maybe someday it will. But today's not the day to push the boundaries. If there is an inkling of indecent expectation in Wolf, I don't want to encourage it. Things are fine the way they are. God forbid he'd mess with that.

Still, I can't help smiling a little when he hands me back my record. I'm excited about popping this on when I get home, exactly like the fancy people. I look around to see if anyone other than me is deriving pleasure from the distinctive blue stripe on the sleeve. Am I fancy now? Maybe I'll buy myself a few beers, and a plant. Where's my stupid insurance money?

The rest of the day rolls by like every other, since I decide to turn off the radio. A whole morning of reminiscing is more than enough. The weird incident involving the pushed tables is similarly pushed aside in my mind, thanks to my lunch-hour distractions and the redundancy of everything that is my life at the shop. When everything is always the same, it's easy to keep the improbable out. What is normal is real, and what is not, is not. I don't really care to understand. That's what I tell myself.

After some errands I go back to the shop, grab my turntable and climb up home. With a few plants added to the floor collection, my new jungle is taking shape. The air soon smells like food; real food, because I am cooking some. Baked potatoes, steamed veggies and sausages. I am a kitchen goddess. My plate, sided by my beer, is placed on the floor before me. Jr. Walker and the All-Stars plays, and it's so delicious on its own that my food automatically tastes a million times better. Musical MSG. I feel pretty damn good.

The sun begins its descent and my mind wanders to the night ahead. I want to try my luck and leave the blinds open and the rolled shirt off my face, that perchance I might be woken by my favourite brand of coffee: sun. Readying myself, I soon hear Eveleen vocalizing her first surges of carnal pleasure. She sounds sincere, at least. Not fake, like in the movies. There is a real rawness to it, like whatever that Shaah-rl guy is doing is really working. They are early tonight. Maybe they have plans later. Or maybe they just couldn't wait. I sit on my bed and listen to them for a while, wondering what it would be like. It's been so long I almost forget. Before I begin to have any suppressed urges released into my own system, I reach for my tumbler and the little pill jar.

I'm on a dock. It's windy and the sky is overcast. My feet are near the edge, overlooking a small waterfall that drops into a turbulent river, directed away with high cement walls. I'm dreaming, and it's strange how aware I am of this fact.

Out of nowhere, Fritz zooms past my legs and jumps into the water. It turns out Fritz can't swim. He sinks. Without thinking, I jump in after him. The cold water envelops my head as I search the waters for him with my arms, and grab hold of his body just before we take the plunge down the waterfall. We sink deep before bobbing out again, riding the fast current down the cement trench, until finally landing in a calm pool. After crawling out, I release Fritz from my tight grasp. He runs off immediately.

In front of me is a museum. Without doors and hardly any walls, its roof rests on large, cylindrical pillars. I walk towards it.

The first area I step into has little glass domes with miniature things inside them displayed in rows on short wooden stands: a miniature gramophone with a brass horn, a rotting piece of organic substance—I'm guessing an animal's stomach or liver, a spool of thread. Why are they keeping this shit behind glass? I try to free the vintage record player, but the glass lid is stuck. I pull, and then I push, but it won't budge, so I kick the stand.

The glass and the gramophone go flying, crashing to the ground and breaking into a million pieces.

"Damn it," I say, looking around to see if anyone saw. But I'm alone. Fleeing the scene, I walk into another section of the museum. This one is dimly lit thanks to its back wall, the whole of which is covered with a glowing photograph. There is the backlit silhouette of a man standing in front of it. He turns and gestures to me.

"Come see this," he says. It's Wolf. I join him and look at the photograph. It is that of a houseplant, in a terra cotta pot, reaching about twice my height. My name is scribbled along the bottom edge of the pot.

"I'd love to own a plant like that with you," he says, putting his arm around my shoulder. My heart accelerates, but I let him. I hear whimpers. Eveleen, somehow cutting through into my dream.

"Do you hear that?" I ask without taking my eyes off the plant.

"Yes. Your neighbour."

"What is she doing here?"

"You're dreaming. Does it matter?"

It doesn't, so I leave Wolf's arm on my shoulders.

"It is a dream," I say. I cannot get hurt here, not physically, or emotionally. Not for real. So I decide to let myself trust him. It's just a small switch in my mind, but it feels big, and liberating. We stand like this, staring at the glowing photograph, listening. After Eveleen reaches a glorious end, I step ahead and clumsily pull the plant out from the photo, wrapping it with both my arms. As it leaves its two-dimensional state, it shrinks to a normal size I can easily hold.

"For you, Wolf." I hold the plant out. Wolf lays his hands over mine, and we both stand there in silence, looking at the plant between us.

# SEVEN

It's Monday. I'm rested but I'm not sure how I feel about my dream. It was so vivid. All that trust bullshit. I push it aside.

It's raining pretty hard, and we all know what happens with broken shoes in the rain. So at lunchtime I decide to skip record exploring and buy myself some new footwear. With a million droplets splattering the sidewalk, my soles join the chorus. Drippity-flap, drippity-flop-drip, drippity-drip-drip-flap-flop. My socks are drenched after one block. It pisses me off, just a little.

Some people have no idea what it's like to be poor, or even just broke. They will never know what it's like to have to just *go without*. To worry about making the rent. To chew without joy, because all there is to eat is rice, rice, and more rice. To endure wet socks and the flapping noises of broken shoes in the rain. To shower with dish soap because there's no more body wash. To put ketchup on everything because it's the only "spice" in the kitchen. To pawn the jewellery inherited from a beloved, deceased grandmother to pay the bills. Bills like boomerangs never flung far enough.

I kick some water out of a puddle.

So what if I know what it's like? Does that make me special? Did I develop any superpowers because of the shit situations I've lived through?

No.

But I must have gained something. There has to be.

I drag my foot, already sopping wet, through another puddle and fling out as much water as I can.

Resilience. And stamina. For this marathon of pain and hopelessness.

Restraint. So much goddamn restraint.

That I have had plenty of.

But pain doesn't care what walk of life you're from. Natural disasters don't strike with discrimination. Nor does the heartbreak of losing a loved one. Divorce and break-ups, illness, the cruelty of others, animal attacks.

Indigestion. Yes, we all get to know the blues one way or another. No one is spared. Even a baby has to go through the trauma of having his skull squished through the birth canal, the discomfort of belly aches, the absolute torture of cutting fresh teeth through tender, pink gums. That baby did nothing to deserve the pain. His soul is as pure as it gets. Clearly, suffering is part of life.

On my way back, I see Wolf under the awning, keeping dry as he smokes. I, on the other hand, am drenched, but I have new shoes. The last of my money has been transformed into canvas and rubber. Wolf sees me and waves.

"Thanks for the plant!" he yells.

"What?"

"Thanks for the plant!" he repeats louder. I had heard him the first time. I just didn't understand what he was talking about. I wave and unlock the shop. The door closes behind me and the little bell hanging above it rings again just as I get to the sink where I plan to wring out my hair.

"Heeey, this is not so bad," Wolf says.

"Oh, hi Wolf. First time here after all these years, huh?"

"Well, I never felt too inclined before. I always thought you hated my guts."

"I hate everyone's guts. It's nothing personal."

"Oh."

"So, you want a coffee?"

"No, well, sure, but, I wanted to say thanks."

"Thanks for what?"

"The plant you left on my counter. I don't know how you got in but it's mighty sweet of you."

"What? No, no no. I didn't give you a plant. Nope. That's … not from me. Ok, so you want a coffee or what? I have to work."

"What do you mean not from you? Your name is written on it."

My head finds its way into my palms and I squeeze my temples. It was a dream. It makes no sense.

"Oh, that's right. Shit. What am I thinking. I left it there, yesterday, by accident. I went shopping for plants, you know? I do that. Sorry, I didn't mean to make you think I was, like, trying to *woo you with gifts* or something. Holy crap, god save me."

"Huh. No, not at all, I just thought it was a really nice gesture. My mistake. Do you want it back?"

"You know what? Yes, please."

Wolf's face falls a little and he turns to leave.

"Wait," I say. "Never mind. Keep it."

He stands at the exit with his hand on the handle, the cold light of the rainy day falling on him through the door's window. He clearly doesn't want some weird pity plant.

"Ok, fine. I did it. I put the plant there this morning before you came in for work. Sorry I lied. I'm not telling you how I did it though. I don't want to get into trouble."

He turns, and I force a fake smile, dropping my eyes, feeling defeated by the situation. When I look back up, he's smiling. He takes a few steps towards me, and I am thankful the counter is between us because I don't want to have to kung-fu his ass.

"As I was saying, then, thanks for the plant, Edie."

"Yup. You're welcome, Wolf." I shuffle around for a take-out cup. "Here, on the house. Enjoy." I pour a coffee and hand it to him. I just want him to leave.

"Wow, full of generosity today. Did you get your insurance money?"

"Actually, no. I should probably call them. Thank goodness this shit job covers my rent."

Wolf listens, chews on his lip as he mulls over something. "You wanna go for dinner with me tonight?"

I almost choke. "Hell, no!"

"Excuse me?"

"I mean, damn. Wolf, you're a nice person. And I'm kind of glad we are talking now, to each other. It's fun to have a not-so-idiot human in my life other than Olive and the gang at the old folks home ..."

Wolf frowns.

"I don't want friends, Wolf, especially not boyfriends, if you know what I mean. I just don't."

"Oh. You're a lesbian?"

"No! What the hell is it with you people. Even if I was. It's nothing that concerns you." My attention shifts to the stuff on the counter. The glass-domed trays need to be pushed a millimetre to the left, and then to the right. The empty tip jar needs to be wiped down. My rag leaves coffee grinds on it, making me sigh.

Wolf grimaces. "What happened to you?"

"Nothing you need to worry about. This is just me, dude. Take it or leave it. I mean, you can stop talking to me if that makes it easier to not ask me out."

"Whoa. Ok. Look, I'm going to go back across the street now and forget this conversation happened."

"No, don't forget it. I'm serious. If we can't talk to each other without somehow me leading you on, then let's not talk. But if you can live with an acquaintance as fucking cold as me, then by all means, I'll keep coming for records."

"Can cold acquaintances eat together?"

His eyes are locked on mine, emotionless. Like he couldn't care less what I answer. I'm not sure what game he's playing, but I can feel the tension retreating. Could he be just a *non-friend* friend?

"Maybe." I say. He smiles and leaves.

Fuck. I should have said no.

At building fifty-one, my mailbox is empty. No cheque. The climb up the stairs is making my ass burn today. My keys land on the counter with a clang and the door swings shut with a bang. The houseplants almost glow in the fiery, low sun. I decide to call my sister.

"Emily Stacks," I say as she picks up the phone.

"Edie!"

"Yup."

"How are you? How's your new apartment? Have you been sleeping?"

"I'm good, I'm good. The loft is ok. Empty, but mine. It's slowly filling up with new plants. And yeah,

I've been sleeping. Thanks again for the help." I remember another part of my dream and my eyes wander along the wall opposite the window. As I feared, there are bits of busted record player on the ground. I must have walked right past it this morning.

"Did you hear what I just said?" Emily says.

"Sorry. What?"

"Fritz almost drowned yesterday. Did you know some dogs can't swim?"

"Fritz?" Hit with a bout of vertigo, I slide down the wall and sit on the floor.

"Yes, but he's fine. He's good for tomorrow's visit."

The words don't quite come.

"Hello? You still there?" she asks.

"Uh, ya. Sorry."

"Edie, are you ok?"

"Ya, I'm fine. Just … Sorry, you were saying Fritz is good to go?"

"Yes."

"Ok. Great. So I'll see you tomorrow. And I'll have your money."

"Oh, there's no rush …"

"Bye." I hang up.

The plant, the busted record player, the drowning dog. The tables pushed up against the wall of the coffee shop. These all happened in my dreams first. Some I made happen. Others I didn't. Fritz, he just jumped. I had no control over that. What a stupid dog. Why would he jump if he can't swim? An eerie feeling comes over me. One of alarm, but also excitement. What does this mean?

The bewildered dizziness soon makes way for possibilities. Can I make any kind of shit happen at will? What would I do next? Then again, what if it's all a fluke, a serendipitous merging of conditions? I'm so eager I can hardly wait for bedtime to test it.

Night finally falls. My water sits undisturbed in its tumbler, the jar of pills on the blanket in front of me, looking guilty. I can almost hear the elfish timbre of the little pink capsules having a good laugh. I pick it up and hold the jar to my ear. Nothing.

I decide to google Luumore. It doesn't show up in any searches.

"Well, that's strange," I mumble, reaching for the pamphlet on the floor by my bed. A small island of half a square kilometre, Luumore has a population of twenty-three. Twenty-fucking-three. I count the farm workers in the picture on the back. They're all there. No more no less.

Eveleen starts. I can't help but wonder what Shaah-rl is doing to her to make it so damn good. Then again, maybe it's all Eveleen. I listen more keenly than I should, a long-forgotten appetite quickening my breath. The clickity-clacking from below is right on time, as are the sewing machines, and the wailing baby. The building is alive. My tongue curls around the pill and hauls it to the back of my throat with the water. Arms spread like wings, I fall back and embrace the oncoming sleep and its inexplicable dreams.

I'm standing behind the counter in my coffee shop.

"How exciting," I say to myself as I look around for anything weird, but everything seems in its place. Maybe this isn't a dream. Have I gotten up already and gone to work? A woman walks in. She wears a Victorian dress with a fur cloak. It's the middle of summer; she must be dying of heat. She orders a petit café, and somehow she's Emily at the same time. How odd. A short espresso in hand, she sits down at a table nearby.

"I'm dreaming!" I yell out at her, as a test. She doesn't flinch.

Jack comes in. Oh, Jack. My favourite jerk. The phone is glued to his ear, his grey hair combed to the side like he's got something to hide, his eyes wandering the walls and dropping to the counter as he gets near. The coins flung seem to take a particularly long time to land, finally resonating with dull clangs on the wooden counter. With hypnotic slowness, I swipe my arm across the surface, and send the coins flying across the room. My hands reach out and grab his head, his big ears poking out between my fingers, and yank his face near mine.

"Hellllloooooo Jackasssssssss!" I smile as the words ooze out of my mouth. His eyes grow large with affront and then fear. My hands release his head as they would a trapped bird, and I feel more satisfied than I have in a long time.

"You want that stupid drink now, Sir?"

Jack runs off, and the overdressed woman follows.

Locking the door behind me out of habit, I leave the shop, and, a few steps later, enter my apartment building.

"I want that cheque."

Convinced that I can will it to appear, I squeeze my eyes shut and imagine an envelope sitting in the little metal box. But when I unlock the trap, it's empty. Fine, I say, stomping up the stairs. Once home, I rummage through a stack of papers piled up on the fridge. Using the edge of the kitchen counter, I rip a blank portion off a utilities bill, and, on it, draw the face of a cheque.

"Pay to the order of Edie Stacks," I mumble as I write. "Five thou …" I scratch it out. "Five million dollars. Signed, Star Insurance." After adding a five-pointed star to the top right corner, making the flagrantly fake cheque look even more like it was crafted by a pre-schooler, I then place the cheque inside an old, used envelope. I tape it shut and run it downstairs to the mailbox where I tuck it in lovingly.

"One can always try."

Back in my hallway, my neighbours' door is slightly ajar. Approaching with light steps, I hear Eveleen and Shaah-rl, their enjoyment a little more subdued, as if quieted by the dreamworld barrier it has to traverse to end up here.

"That's right, it's just a dream," I repeat to myself, my curiosity compelling me closer. My fingers touch the door and push it open a bit more. I peek in. Their loft resembles mine, though it has more furniture, and fewer plants. The sun is beaming in, dust particles meandering in the honeyed glow like miniature fireflies. Beyond my range of view comes some heavy breathing, and a soft squeaking of a bed. I stick my head in a little more, and my eyes find them. They are sideways to me, and fully dressed, though parts of their clothing dangle off them, exposing various slices of skin. A thigh, a shoulder, a breast. I watch, transfixed by the scene, like a painting rich in colour and sensation; the rhythm of Eveleen's heaving, the rolling movement of the head hidden behind her thigh, the hands on her haunches, the fingers clutching and releasing her flesh, over and over, almost cat-like. Eveleen turns and locks her glossy eyes on mine. She smiles.

I'm going to die, I think to myself, embarrassed to the bone. Eveleen releases her grip from the edge of the bed and beckons me to her with a curling finger. My heart stops. In a fear-stricken daze, I back up, close the door in front of me with a soft click, and turn to my own loft which I enter as fast as I can.

There are only so many square feet in my loft, and pacing soon makes me feel trapped. Sensual and obscene thoughts plague me. I'm hot to trot with both fear and lust. I wonder how to wake myself up. I step out on the balcony and look below. Wolf is having a smoke under the awning. He looks up and waves. Fuck. I retreat inside and fall onto my bed, squeezing my eyelids shut.

"Come on, come on…"

I listen to the sounds permeating the walls, gentle, muffled.

Lying still, stubbornly self-denying, I finally drift into a sleep within my sleep.

# EIGHT

Being woken by my sunshine-coffee and rising to a fresh, new day is my joie de vivre. It is an unspeakable blessing that I cherish more than what most people are willing to suffer for: friendship, family, new clothes and gadgets, sex, art, even music. My priorities might be skewed, but they are mine and I wear them proudly. Coming in second are all the other little joys, and I think it is well understood that in my life they are, in fact, little. Still, they make life all the more worthwhile, and I've always known to appreciate them. Sure I complain, but I've never wanted to buy an early ticket out of here, if you know what I mean.

Waking refreshed is the greatest pleasure. It's nighttime that has taken a weird turn, and it has left me with many questions.

Not leading me to comfortable oblivion anymore, it is a realm where I now feel acutely aware. Some parts of my dreams are strange and ludicrous, the way we expect them to be, but other parts feel much too real and believable. Just as real as the fabric of my sheets I now roll between my fingers, or the freshness of the air I'm pulling into my lungs. Sometimes it's hard to tell which is real, and which is not.

I look at my phone, and I'm pleased to realize it's Tuesday. A visit to the old folks' home will keep my mind off this craziness for a few hours.

It's not quite 8 a.m. by the time I get to Emily's. She works from home and sleeps in every single day, so I am remorseless when I assault her with both the buzzer and phone calls.

"Fritz heard you way before I did," she tells me, rubbing the sleep from her eyes. It looks to me as if she needs an east-facing window.

With the usual satisfaction that comes from acquitting dues, I hand over the twenty dollar bill I'd been keeping safe in the fridge's otherwise empty butter compartment. Emily pushes it down into her pocket without looking at it, affectionately studying my wandering gaze instead. She always looks at me right in the face, and she's the only person whose eyes I can't stand to look into.

At the Cedar Residence, a few of the elderly are up and about, playing cards or staring out windows. Most are sleeping right there in the common room, having gotten up from their beds before realizing they weren't quite done.

"Hi Edie," a nurse says. She crouches to pet Fritz. "You two are early today."

"Yup. Just looking forward to seeing Olive."

"She just woke up. You can go see her."

Through the slightly open door, I watch her before going in. She is at a small desk, reading a magazine. Her shaky hand keeps rubbing down her thigh, as if to wipe off sweat, or to smoothen the wrinkles out of her long, flowered skirt. Unhooked from his leash, Fritz trots in.

"Oh!" She lets him jump up on her lap and turns her shaky little head towards me. "Come on in." She waves me in and turns back to her magazine.

"Good morning, Olive."

"These models are so incredibly skinny. They mustn't be getting vey much to eat."

I climb onto her bed and sit cross-legged facing her hunched back. Her face bent low near her fashion magazine, she flips a page with interest.

"Do you remember your dreams, Olive?"

"Oh," she says, her attention pulled away from the anorexic-looking models. She shifts her body and drapes an elbow over the back of her chair, staring at the ground in front of her for a moment before looking up at me with sparkling eyes. "I used to want to be a tightrope walker. Isn't that wild?" Her body rattles with gentle laughter.

"Oh, that sounds amazing. Did you end up doing it?"

"Almost."

That's all she says, her gaze dropping back to the floor. I know she had worked as a care-taker for young children, and that, though she married, never had kids of her own. She came from a time when women could only aspire to be teachers, nurses, or housewives. That's it. Some broke the mould, though. I wonder what got in the way of Olive's tightrope dreams. Her husband is my first guess.

"Olive, what I meant is: do you remember your *sleeping* dreams."

"Ooh, those dreams. Well, sometimes, yes, I do."

"Do you sometimes realize you're dreaming while you're dreaming?"

"Ooh, that's called lucid dreaming, my dear. A whole bunch of kids were doing it on purpose in the sixties. The trick is ..." Olive stops talking as she opens a drawer from her desk and pulls out a comb with her bony, wrinkly hands, passing it to me. Her eyes are wide, her smile warm. I inch over to the edge of the bed and take it.

"The trick is?" I invite her to continue.

"The trick is with what, dear?"

"Lucid dreaming. You were saying: the trick is ..."

She talks as I pass the comb through her grey strands.

"Oh." She thinks for a moment. "Yes, the trick is to stay calm. If you get too excited, you'll wake yourself right up." Her hands jerk upwards, and gently land in her lap again. "Do you know how to check?"

"Check for what?"

"Check if you're really dreaming," she says in a whisper. Her face turns just enough for me to see her eyes grow big with excitement.

"I don't. I should, shouldn't I? My dreams seem so real sometimes."

"Well, then, check the clocks, the light switches, and your hands. You'll know for sure, then." She smiles, happy to bestow knowledge.

"How did you become so cool, Olive?"

"I don't know. I just am I guess!"

After a few minutes of quiet combing, she returns to her favourite subject.

"You have a husband yet?" She sounds hopeful.

"Not since last week." Every visit, she asks me. "There's more to life than getting married, you know. Times have changed."

"Oh, you think that now, but when you have a partner, a real partner"—she strains to look up at me —"you feel like you can take on the world."

"Like a team."

"That's right! A team. A *winning* team." She pats my hand, her way of telling me to stop. She turns completely in her chair. "You're a beautiful young lady,

Edie. And so smart. I don't know why you want to stay all alone."

"Maybe I'm not courageous like you. I couldn't ever dream of tightrope walking."

"Well, that was just a wild idea anyway. Tell me." She looks at me, joy illuminating her face. "What is it *you* dream of?"

I sigh a long sigh and stare out at the trees through the window. "Not having to worry about paying my rent would be good. Maybe someday I could own a car, and just drive. Explore the wilderness. Maybe … I could run a plant nursery."

"Oh! Yes, you love plants! That sounds perfect. And you don't see a man beside you when you dream these things?"

"I don't really dream these things, Olive. I've just been so bored and frustrated with life these last few years. I don't know. I'm just trying to get by. I certainly don't need someone bringing more turbulence into my life. More hurt."

"Oh, poor heart. A partner should bring stability, and love. Obviously you haven't met the right one."

"Ok, Olive."

Fritz and I take a detour along a meandering brook on the way back to my sister's. The birds are chirping frantically against the breeze, their form hidden by the greenery no matter how much the wind rattles the branches. That sums up what I want. To sing my song, but to stay completely hidden. To be left alone. I like the idea of a team, I must admit; but I also know how rare and improbable it would be to meet someone who fits the bill. My picky-ass bill. I don't think I could ever trust someone enough to even let them try.

When I get home, I go for the mailbox as I usually do, remembering my little experiment only as I'm about to open it. The key pauses half-turn. Suddenly I'm scared of discovering the truth. My breath quickens.

The tiny metal door squeaks as I pull it open. There's my envelope. With a trembling hand, I pull it out. The scotch tape is folded over the ripped edges, just as I placed it last night. I pick at it, and pull it off. My fingers reach in for the rectangular paper.

It's a cheque. A real one. And it's written out to me, from Star Insurance. Five million dollars. My legs go weak, and I have to hang on to the small counter under the mailboxes to not fall to my knees. My lungs tighten and I'm having a hard time breathing.

"Ee-dee," Eveleen says as she walks into the entrance. I jolt up to my feet.

"I slipped," I say.

"Oh." She nods, a doubtful frown at her brow. Then she smiles, a naughty twinkle appearing in her eyes. "You want to come for a visit, to take dinner wit me and Shaah-rl tonight?"

The idea of being alone with them makes me instantaneously nervous.

"I have plans for dinner, I'm sorry," I lie.

"You are sure? I make a good crêpe suzette. I put flame on it. It's very hot. You can *watch*."

My face twitches up at her as she emphasizes the last word. She looks at me with knowingness in her smile. She knows I spied on them. But she can't possibly.

"It's nice seeing you. I really gotta …" I point to the stairs with my thumb and turn, hurrying up in case she follows.

My keys are tangled.

"Damn it!" I look to my right. I hear Eveleen's footsteps echo from the stairwell. The correct key finally isolated, I jam it in and jiggle it furiously until it clunks open. In the safety of my loft, the door closed behind me, my keys on the counter, I zombie my way to the bed and sit down with the cheque in my lap.

"What does this mean? What does this mean?"

*It means you're rich*, I say to myself with a bit of humour.

"I'm rich!" Laughter, then tears, burst out of my face.

I'm thoroughly confused all the way to the bank. I decide to do the transaction with a teller. With an amount like this, it's not worth the risk of losing it to the fingers of brainless machines.

"This is quite the amount," the woman says, eyeing me suspiciously.

"I know! I'm shocked."

Honesty is the best way to lie.

"My place burned down," I confess. "I didn't expect so much insurance. But I'll take it! I've always wanted a TV."

She frowns.

"I mean, I've always wanted a curved, smart, 4D TV. You know, just to be different from all the other flatscreens I had around the house. In like, every room. They all burned. Nine. TVs."

She pinches her lips together and leaves with my cheque. When she comes back, she has someone with her. A financial advisor who smiles like a car salesman, his skin fake-and baked to an unnatural bronze, his teeth too white, the chain around his neck too gold. He extends his hand to shake mine. When that awkwardness is over, he offers to make an appointment with me to discuss investments. Sure, I say. But today I just want to deposit my money. He leaves us.

"Would you like to take some out? Seeing as we just confirmed your cheque is valid," the teller says in a tone that suggests she would have rather discovered it was counterfeit. "You don't have to wait for it to be cleared."

"No, thank you. But could you tell me how much I can access with my card?"

She gives me jargon and numbers. I hear: thousands and thousands. Every day.

A receipt and a fresh card: that's what I get. I rub my thumb over the little golden oak leaf in the upper right-hand corner of the card; the symbol for *you're loaded*, I suppose. I shove it in my raggedy wallet before I thank her and leave.

I can say one thing, the air smells different when you're filthy rich.

The door opens and closes soundlessly as I walk into the Spin Factory. Wolf is placing some records into some bins. He turns to me.

"You need a bell above your door," I say.

"I heard you just fine." He smiles.

"That's because you're in between songs."

Wolf frowns when he sees I'm just standing there, twisting my fingers together.

"What's up? Are you ok?" He walks towards me. I try to stop him with my eyes but it doesn't work. He stops ten inches from me. "Is there something wrong?"

"No." I take a deep breath. "You wanna do that food thing later?"

"You mean dinner?"

I clear my throat. "Yes. Um, like, cold acquaintances eating together."

He nods, amused.

"Only I pay," I add. At his concerned look, I tell him, "The insurance came through, big time."

We go to a well-lit, greasy spoon a few blocks away. The last thing I want is to show off, or, god forbid, create a romantic mood. I just want to share a little bit. I want to say to someone, "Hey, this is fucking great. Share a fry with me." As much as I love Emily, she's more a sister than a friend, if that makes any sense. We aren't close. We never tell each other anything really personal. In truth, I only have Olive. I'll have to bring her a gift next time I visit.

"You look better. You've been getting some sleep, I suppose," Wolf says as he reaches into the family-sized portion of fries sitting between our respective paper placemats.

"I have. Super weird sleep, though."

"How is that?"

I bite my lip, feeling I've spoken too fast.

"Maybe this was a bad idea."

"What?"

"This dinner."

"It's fine, Edie. I assure you, we are not friends. You eat your fries over there. I'll eat mine here. I couldn't care less. We're celebrating money." He munches without sound, his lips politely closed.

"I've been lucid dreaming," I tell him.

"Shit. Ok." He throws another fry into his mouth, smiles, and looks around the restaurant, pretending he doesn't give a crap. He has to be pretending. He's humouring me. So I let him, for now.

"I know that I'm dreaming while I'm dreaming."

"I know what lucid dreaming is," he says.

"Of course you do."

I pop a fry into my mouth and go to speak, but, self-conscious about my manners, I finish chewing first. "You ever had them?"

"Only a few times. They weren't fully lucid either. Just like, glimpses of lucidity."

"Oh. I've been having them ever since I started sleeping again."

"So, maybe it's the supplements?"

"Huh?"

"The supplements you said you were taking. Maybe there's something in them that's triggering it. Feeding some weird hormone in your brain, or however the hell it works."

Of course, the pink pills have to be causing the lucid dreams. But drugs don't make five-million-dollar cheques appear out of thin air.

"Perhaps, yes."

"So, you've flown yet?"

"What do you mean?"

"Isn't that the first thing we all want to try? Fly?"

I shrug.

"You should take advantage. This is really cool. Play with it, have fun."

I catch a glimpse of something then. A spark of clarity, a single pulse of a stroboscope, momentarily shows me the truth: the person sitting across the table, this human named Wolf, is a friend. It's grounding.

"Thanks."

"For what?"

"For the idea. I'm going to fly."

# NINE

Night comes around. I see my little jar of supplements is almost empty. I'm reticent to buy more; getting addicted was never part of the plan. Not that I crave them. But I do need them to bury the neighbours.

I shouldn't forget: I'm rich now. It sounds unreal in my mind. I haven't said it out loud yet but I imagine it'll sound just the same, if not weirder. The money's in the bank, and a hundred and one different ways of how to get away from building fifty-one are popping into my head. One of them is to quit my job and move to an uninhabited island with a pet monkey named Gurt. But I don't want to kill prey with my own hands or wipe with a leaf, so I push that idea aside. I don't really understand what this money represents. I can't even imagine what I might do with it. I've always lived hand to mouth.

Like clockwork, the building comes alive an hour before midnight. The idea that I could ever sleep through such a ruckus is humorous. Plucked from the jar and admired with gratitude, the pink pill dives into my mouth.

The morning sun crashes brightly onto my bed, heating the skin on my face. My eyes open and I see Fritz sitting at the base of my bed, staring at me.

"Fritz, boy. What are you doing here?"

He comes up to me for pets. I tousle his ears and put my feet onto the floor. I hear giggling.

"Who's here?" I say under my breath. Following the voices to the bathroom, I push open the door to find my sister and Wolf, laughing as they fix each other's hair.

Wolf has a light mauve pouf on his head, seeming to have come straight off Marie-Antoinette's own coconut. Emily is wearing a white one. Both of them have a whole bunch of Lego pieces tucked in above the first bump, like a crown. They look at me and laugh even harder.

"What the hell are you guys doing?"

"We're playing! You wanna?" says Wolf. Emily is holding in her giggles so doggedly, she squirms like she needs to pee. Her face is bright red.

"Breathe, Emily," I tell her. And she bursts into laughter. I walk away from them, back into the main room of my loft. I look around. Something feels off. Olive said to check my hands. I hold them up and count my fingers. The sight of six on each sends shivers down my back. I look back into the bathroom. Wolf is lying in the empty bath tub, smoking a cigarette. Emily sits on the lid of the toilet, reading a thick book. Fritz rubs up against my leg. When I look down, he's become a big tabby cat. A dull, reddish glow travels from one of its eyes to the other, like marbles lit from the inside.

"Ok," I tell myself. "I'm dreaming. Now what?" The conversation from the night before echoes in my mind.

*So, have you flown yet?*

My feet planted firmly on the floor, I take a few moments to think. Am I sure I'm dreaming? I look back in the bathroom. Wolf and Emily are gone. So is Fritz. I look back to my hands, both of them still enhanced with extra, blurry fingers. Fuck it. I push open the balcony doors and climb onto the ledge of the wooden railing.

*I'm dreaming. I'm dreaming. I can do this.*

My eyes shut tight, I jump. And fall. Before I hit the ground, I force myself to look.

*Just fly, dammit!*

My pyjama pants flapping, my T-shirt pasted to my chest, I'm propelled forward, upward. I am flying, my arms out like a fucking airplane. I howl so loud, my body tilts, and my mind flickers; the jolt of emotion is waking me up. A fear seizes me: I'm going to crash. So what? The worse that can happen is that I'll wake up, I think to myself, though part of me isn't so sure I would emerge unscathed. Thankfully, the pills are stronger than my excitement, it seems, and they keep me under. My body returns to a parallel position. I'm flying, and it's awesome.

Once past my street, the buildings start to all look the same, meshing into a condensed platform of colourful Lego blocks. Funny, I think to myself. The wind feels fresh on my skin. I let my eyes close to enjoy the sensation better. When I open them, I am standing outside a big house in the suburbs.

"It looks big," I tell Olive, who is standing beside me. This is stupidly strange, but I go with it. I want to see inside this house.

Wooden floors, big windows, huge rooms separated with actual walls and doors. The back yard is taken over by a big pool, a little shed tucked in the back. Cedar bushes fence the perimeter.

"I like it," I say. I walk out to the edge of the water, sit down, and put my feet in. My body slips in next, and, slowly, the blue water engulfs me completely.

I wake up. Again. Rubbing my temples, I think back. For a lucid dream, it sure led me wherever it pleased. The flying, though, I did that. I'll have to tell Wolf.

My feet on the sun-warmed floor, I make my way to the bathroom. A light-mauve wig sits on the lid of the toilet.

A chunk of my dream again manifested in my real life. And why would that craziness end just because I've gotten something I want out of it? I can't just *shut it down* with my millions of dollars. This is bigger, and wilder, than money. What's worrisome is that I can't seem to control what transfers over. Actually, all of it is worrisome, and I wonder how I am not losing my mind. Or maybe this is me losing my mind, calm in the midst of insanity.

Picking up the wig, I notice the Legos are not Legos at all but small pieces of cake. I smell one. Vanilla. I throw the pouf into the bathtub.

The door to the Spin Factory is kept open with a door stopper, letting the fresh summer air in. The second my foot crosses the threshold, Wolf comes at me.

"Edie, you won't believe what happened."

"Dude, I flew!" I cut in.

"Oh! That's even better news! I'm so happy for you." Wolf puts his hands on my shoulders and gently pushes me against the counter.

"What the hell are you doing?" I ask.

He moves closer, until his face is an inch from mine.

"Something amazing happened," he says, looking into my eyes. He threads his fingers into my hair and kisses me.

My knee is ready to make him cry, but his lips are soft and he smells like dessert. A test with my tongue confirms: he tastes like vanilla.

Surprising myself, I kiss him back, at first with slow, gustatory delight, and then with mouthfuls of scrumptious delectation. I realize I'm starving for cake. I wrap my arms around him, and he lifts me onto the counter, climbing up after me.

"Edie," he says in a panting whisper between kisses, "there's this amazing record I want you to hear." He squirms in closer. Too close. He's good to go, and so am I.

"Edie," he says again in my ear as his hand explores my chest. Chills pierce through my heat. "Have you ever heard of Gamelan music?"

The record screeches to a halt. We are making out on his store counter in broad daylight. People are shopping, and he's whispering music gibberish in my ear. I'm dreaming. Of course. I would never do this.

I place my hand over his face and push it back as I scan the room. Hanging on a wall beam across from us is an analog clock. It should be eight in the morning. But my eyes are screwy and I can't read the time. I squeeze them shut and open them again. The clock hands are warped.

"Am I dreaming?" I ask Wolf, pulling my hand away from his face.

"Most certainly," he confirms. "Look at this." And he shows me his index. A small flame bursts out of its tip.

"Good. Then let's do this right." I jump down and lead him by the hand towards the back. A black door on the right leads to a dim closet, a rod full of winter coats, and no windows. One by one, I toss the winter coats to the ground. I nudge Wolf towards them. He sits down and leans back on his elbows. He has a strange twinkle in his eye, a sort of awareness, as if he is the one having the wet dream and not the other way around. How real it all seems. The way he looks at me then, in any real life scenario, would've thrown a wrench in the gears, but I ignore it. I'm too famished.

I strip, and have my way with him.

I wake up yet again. This time I linger in bed, quite pleased with how I handled my last dream. I stretch slowly like a baby spider, if baby spiders could stretch. I swing my legs over the side of my bed. Doubt pinches me. My hands—I look at them. They have five fingers each. I look at my phone. The white numbers glow: 6 a.m. That makes me smile. Even with sleeping pills, my circadian rhythm is on point. I pinch myself. I have good reason to believe I am really awake this time, and blow my worries away with a big, well-satisfied sigh.

Down at the coffee shop, I serve customers with renewed zeal. I dial up my boss, who is much like the evil hand in the Mr. Gadget cartoons; he surely has a face, but it is one I never see. His name is Todd and he owns twelve other shops in this city alone. He doesn't run a franchise. It's a mom-and-pop chain, he says, and he wants it to feel that way. I always figured it's because the other shops are doing so well that he doesn't bother to check on what's happening with mine. The numbers show up in the bank, the orders are made, the shop is run. That's all that matters. Todd is a coffee shop slumlord who get as little involved as possible.

"Todd," I say when he answers the phone. "Edie here, from Pine Street. Yes, I'm good thank you; good enough to quit ... Yes, that's right ... I understand ... Sure, I can do that."

Content with my lot, I scribble "help wanted" with a sharpie onto a white piece of paper. The sign taped onto the window, I look through, across to the Spin Factory. I haven't considered what it would be like to give up lunch-time crate digging. I guess I'll just have to go out of my way and come here to shop every so often. It would be nice of me to let Wolf know I won't be his neighbour anymore.

Though I never walk in and say a big hello like an extravert might, my greeting is particularly hushed today. At the sight of Wolf, the heat of my dream comes back in a flash, reddening my cheeks. Feeling out of place, I find some records and start flipping, my eyes straining to focus on the band names I'm not really reading and the album art I don't really see. Wolf appears beside me, leaning with his elbow on the next row, peeking under my gaze.

"Hey," he says.

I give him a brief look, nod, and continue flipping.

"Are you ok?" He touches my arm, a grin at his lips. He knows something. Oh shit, what sort of mess have I made? Keep it together, Edie, I tell myself.

"I'm fine, Wolf. How about you?" I keep moving down the aisle.

"Great, actually. I slept so good last night."

By this time I've flipped through two rows without noticing one record, two rows away from his touchy-feely hands and the knowing look in his eyes. I keep flipping. He inches closer.

"I've found the weirdest music. I'm sure you're going to dig it."

On a whim, I say, "Let me guess. Gamelan."

"Whoa! How did you know?" His face scrunches up and he pouts, looking around him to see if he left the record lying around somewhere. I flip my way down the aisle at an amazing speed. He waits for me on the opposite side.

"Classical, huh?"

I'm flipping through the classical records. It doesn't matter. I don't stop. I plan on flipping all the way to the goddamn door.

"Look." He shows me the record: psychedelic purple and pink swirls, white explosive stars, and intricate black line work running across its sleeve. "Gamelan is Indonesian instrumental music. A bit meditative but weird enough to be interesting."

"Thanks, I'll take it." I grab the record and walk to the cash register, happy to have an excuse to get out. Behind the counter, he takes my card and slips it into the debit machine.

"I'm sorry I touched your arm. I know you said cold acquaintances. But, last night ..."

"What? What *last night?*"

"Just ... a dream I had. Sorry, I'm being weird. Never mind, ok? Here's your record. I hope you like it."

Awkward silence. I wish I had let him speak. I may have found out if he dreamt of sex in a closet. Did I mess with his dream by involving him in mine? The silence is too long. I take the record from his hands and leave.

My earlier enthusiasm gone, the rest of the afternoon is even more morose than usual. Jack comes in. The second I see his stupid face I'm whipping up his ridiculous drink, and it's in front of him before he can even consider basic social exchange. His five dollar tip is a joke to me now, and I harrumph loudly, repressing the urge to chuck it at the back of his head as he walks away.

What I don't expect is someone applying for my job so quickly. A cute redhead, with lots of freckles, and big, green eyes. May. That's her name. She is taking a year off university and wants a non-demanding job.

"You got it," I say.

A twinge of jealously pierces my chest when I think she might meet Wolf. She'll probably meet Wolf. And buy records. He'll think she's cute, that's for sure. Look at her. And she's so friendly, they'll hit it off right away. This is a good thing, I think to myself. I might as well get out of the way as fast as I can.

"I got what?"

"The job, silly head."

"You didn't even look at my résumé."

"I don't need to look at your *résumé*. You're in uni, smarty pants."

"Um, ok then. When do I start?"

"How about I show you around right now, and tomorrow we work together, and then Friday you're on your own." My mind fast-forwards to a near-future me, rubbing my hands together like a villain, tip-toeing the hell away from this godforsaken place.

She agrees, so that's what we do.

"The cups are here, the rags are there, the beans, they're good for two weeks once the bag is opened; the grinds, good for four hours. That's if you want fresh and not stale. Really, though, it's up to you. Espresso machine, we'll cover that one tomorrow; stuff to wash the floor with is back there; the bathroom, and the accounting"—I cough—"we'll do in the morning. We'll cover orders and bank runs at the same time. I'll give Todd your number. Here's his. You can call him afterwards if you have any questions."

"Whew, this is a lot of stuff to remember. Usually people get trained longer than just ... ten minutes."

"Really? Like where?" I'm feeling slightly cocky.

"Well, I worked at the library one summer."

"Ah well, yes, books are a whole other world, missy. This is coffee! You'll be fine." I wait for her to leave.

"Should I go now?"

"Yes."

"Oh, ok. But you'll work with me tomorrow, right?"

"That's right! See? That's much more than ten minutes. Just like your big-time library."

"Um, ok. I'll see you tomorrow then."

"Seven sharp! We open at eight."

She nods and smiles as she makes her way out.

"Well, that was easy."

I flip the chairs onto the tables and sweep the floor, looking outside every so often. The Spin Factory windows look black thanks to the bright sun, and, even though I squint, I can't see inside at all.

# TEN

My apartment is drenched in the waning sunlight, the rays potentially blinding depending on where you stand. The Gamelan record placed with the few others, I flop onto my bed and reach to the floor. There's one pill left in the little pill jar. I haven't decided if I will buy more. Do I need more? If I stop taking them, will the lucid dreaming stop? Do I want it to? I've gotten enough out of it. A shitload of money. And I flew. What more does a person need, really?

If I let the pills run out, but move quickly, I won't lose too much sleep. I could always sleep during the day, since I won't need to get up for work, but I would hate that. It's like living upside down, head in the dirt, feet in the air. Still, I could do it for the time it takes to get a new place.

The water turned on and the curtain pulled just wide enough to let me through, I step into the shower. And scream. The purple wig and two dozen cigarette butts are bunched in the drain, blocking the flow. My mind jumps to the hot sex with Wolf, and my heart almost stops with anxiety. What if it was as real as this wig? How could it not be? I lift the purple ball of hair with the tips of my fingers and fling it out.

These dreams are messing with my life. Tonight, I won't do anything. I'll park my dream-self on a bench by the beach, and watch the waves roll in, all night. Nothing to cause ripples in my actual life. That's the important thing now. No ripples. That, and finding a house as soon as possible. Maybe that's what I'll do in my sleep. I'll pluck myself a house from the strange ether of possibilities.

As soon as the tap dancing starts, the baby wails, the sewing machines release their jackhammers, and Eveleen erupts into her song of carnal bliss, I'm already punching out, diving deep into a world of wakeful sleep —one where I make things happen in real life, whether I want to or not.

I don't emerge on a bench by the beach. I'm at a pool party. There are bodies everywhere, standing around with drinks. Shirtless guys line the patio stones at one end of the pool, and at the other, girls in bikinis are diving in one by one. The water is murky with orange alphabet soup. Behind me are patio doors leading into a big rec room, which is just as crowded, only the room is quite dark in contrast. I head inside.

Blue lights glow from the corners, giving the room an eerie, pool-water vibe, minus the tomato soup. Wine glasses hang above a bar, glints of blue light reflecting off them and flitting as you walk by. Black leather couches are scattered around the room, each filled with laughter and drinks, music muffling the sound. The Doors, *Riders on the Storm*. Amongst them are couples, French kissing, limbs interlaced, clearly unabashed by their public canoodling. At the far left corner is a door, which leads to some stairs. I take them.

The first landing presents a big open room, with a kitchen at one end, a large TV at the other, and a few pillars in between. The back wall is made of glass, with doors opening to a small balcony overlooking the yard and pool. I climb another flight of stairs.

Entering one of the bedrooms, I realize now that I'm looking for a bathing suit, filled with a sudden urge to jump into the murky soup-pool with the other girls. Having pulled numerous costumes out of the closet, I grumble unhappily at the one I've put on: a crocheted, flimsy thing I'd never really wear. Just then a man enters the room.

Surprised, and at the same time not, I know he's the owner of the house. It dawns on me that this is the house I'm to pluck from the ether. I face him in the weird bathing suit, showing way too much cleavage, way too much of everything, and shake his hand.

"Hello, Sir." I smile. I figure I should get on his good side. Besides, being friendly is much easier here, in dreamland. "Your house, is it for sale?"

"No."

"But it could be?" I raise my eyebrows at him, smiling. His eyes sweep over my top, back and forth, left to right, as if he is trying to read something off me.

"I'd like to buy it." I hesitate a little and take a step closer. I'm not too sure what I'm doing, but I feel urged along, as if my dream has a mind of its own. It's securing me a home.

"Where would I go?" he asks, looking up from my chest.

"Is your mother still alive?"

"No."

"Sister?"

"Frances."

"Yes. She needs you right now," I suggest, taking another tiny step closer.

"No, she doesn't. She's in San Francisco, peeling fish."

"Sir, I have papers you can sign right now. You'll make lots of money." I wave the papers I'm suddenly holding in my hands. There's something printed on there, too fuzzy to read. It doesn't matter. We're making a deal.

"I'm already rich. Did you see my house? Anyway, you can't make me. I wear size fourteen shoes."

He stands still, his eyes dropping again to my bikini top. I step closer still.

"What's your name?"

"Bob."

Bob needs to be convinced that he's selling his house. All he needs is a tiny crocheted convincing.

Maybe there's another way. Maybe there are a million other ways. But I know one that is quick and efficient. I know it's wrong, but the option opens up so naturally, it's hard to not take the bait. The dream knows what I want, and I know I can get what I want, with just a little *canoodling*. Nothing extravagant. Though uncharacteristic today, it's not like I haven't pulled such a manoeuvre in the past. A lifetime ago.

It's not real, I whisper to myself.

I shudder as I take his hands in my hands and place them on my scantily covered breasts. He gives a god-awful chuckle. I place the paper across my collarbone. While one hand still kneads, the other signs, and, without raising the pen off the paper, he lifts his chin to look at me. Eyes are so easy to read if you take the time to look people in the face. Bob has an evil glimmer in his. He has fulfilled his part of the bargain, his eyes say, and now it's my turn.

"Shit." I yank the paper away. He drops the pen. We stare at each other, just for a tiny moment, but a moment that costs me. As I twist towards the door, Bob grabs my shoulders with brick-heavy hands. I slip out, but only manage to take one step away before his hands catch my waist. He pulls me in. One arm wraps around me, and then the other. I'm thrashing, but I've not the strength to break free from his body lock. His cologne burns my nose, his shirt rough against my cheek as he squeezes me tighter. The straps of my top are tugged loose and a pleased grunt rises from his chest. Memories rush in, weakening me. My mouth opens to scream but nothing comes out.

Helpless and overpowered, i feel panic swelling, filling every crevice. A wave of desperation finally bursts through my tightly shut eyelids, rushing down in salty rivulets over the hills of my cheeks.

"Let. GO!"

"Stop squirming, you little whore." He holds me tighter as he yanks down my bikini bottom.

The words I want to yell are stuck in my throat. My fists pound with no force. I feel his erection against my pelvic bone, as hard as his heart of stone. He pulls me tighter against it, and my stomach turns. His fingers dig into my arms, my sides. This is a fucking nightmare.

The thought sinks in through the dread, like a ball of lead in a tumultuous sea. It hits the ocean floor with a thud. A nightmare. But I'm still lucid. I have steering power, just the same. Nothing's changed. He pushes us towards the bed. Every muscle in my body is tensed, yet

I can't free myself. He's everywhere, like an octopus. And I'm exposed, vulnerable, accessible.

My teeth. My teeth are sharp. My teeth are sharp as a lion's. My teeth are sharp as a lion's and I eat fuckers like Bob for breakfast. The backs of my thighs hit the edge of the mattress, and, just as he's about to tip us over, I throw my head forward, clamping my open mouth onto his bicep. I bite hard, with all the dreamworld sinew I can muster, and pull back a chunk of bloody meat in my clenched teeth. Blood gushes down his arm from the deep-red gouge I carved. He roars. His arms slacken, and I wriggle out, running without looking back.

But my legs are heavy, heavy the way dreams make them. In slow motion, I trudge, the fear of being grabbed from behind clawing the back of my skull. I run, too slowly, with gravity pulling down each of my steps. Glue under the soles of my feet, I clump down the stairs and finally reach the back wall of glass. I push open the doors and jump off the balcony, into the pool of rust-coloured soup.

Honey sunlight caresses me awake. Staring at the ceiling, I lie for a while. Escaping the nightmare is not as much a relief as it should be. It feels too close, too real. I remember my dreams so vividly now, I don't even have to try. Waking life is just a continuation of my sleeping life, and vice versa. A smooth transition from one world to the next, like an unending length of ribbon that I can follow, in and out, through night and day. So much so that I'm not surprised at all to find tomato soup caked in my hair, and a piece of paper crumpled in my hand. Under the blankets, I'm naked. Grateful to emerge otherwise intact, I get up.

After washing the evidence out, I slide into a pair of jeans, the back pocket of which carries the folded piece of soup-stained paper. I pull it out to make sure it hasn't transformed into a phone bill. But it's still the promise to purchase, inscribed with Bob's signature, and mine. After a long sigh and a shudder, I fold it up and tuck it back in.

When I make it down to the shop, May is already waiting at the door.

"Hey," I say.

"Good morning." She beams at me. I show her in and turn on the lights, leading her to the alarm system I should be setting every day but don't. At least I still remember the code, which I tell her as I point dismissively to the number pad. She pulls out a notebook and pen and jots it down.

"Wow," I say, stepping into the office at the back of the store. The desk is piled with papers that I have obviously just chucked there and forgotten. I regret the promise to show her how to do the accounting. She seems smart. I'm sure she would have figured it out on her own at some point.

"There's a bit of catching up to do, because I haven't done it in … a few days. It can get confusing, especially when you fall behind."

"Clearly." She cringes at my mess.

She seems more prepared for my rushed directives today, taking notes every so often. She excavates a chair from under a mound of junk and attempts to sit.

"Whoa!" I say. "No, no. Tackle that later, little May. I want to get this training over with."

She stops midway and stands back up. She thinks I'm rude.

"I thought we were working together all day?"

"Sorry, something big came up." Thinking back, I touch my shirt's high neckline and wonder if I should be afraid of real-life Bob. If my nightmare revealed anything true about his person, then I must conclude that he's violent. No amount of demureness will change that.

May clears her throat. I shoot her a half smile.

And with only half my mind on the rest of the tasks, we continue.

By late morning, we've gone over most of everything and have served a number of clients.

"You're all set," I tell her. "I've got to go."

"Ok, I think I'll survive. Thanks so much, Edie."

"Sure. And don't put that tip jar away. As you know, the coffee shop doesn't pay much, so the tips are really helpful. By the end of the week you'll have enough to pay for part of your groceries."

"Oh, that's great, but I have lots of savings. I don't actually need to work. I just think it's healthy."

I chuckle at her privileged morality. The money in my bank account hasn't been there long enough to make such ideas anything other than alien.

"Say, you don't need an apartment do you?" I offer, knowing full well it's wrong to do so. "I'm moving out, and my place is right next door."

"That sounds convenient, but no thanks. I'm happy with my place in the Green Square."

"That's a pricey neighbourhood."

"Not really."

There's a short silence, during which May drifts further and further away from our plane of mutual understanding. Before she's completely out of sight, I throw her a lifeline.

"The store across the street. You might want to check it out. It's a great way to spend a lunch break."

"Oh, ok. Sure." She nods, then picks up a rag, ready to get *healthy*.

One look at May and you can tell she has her shit together. Her hair is clean, her eyes are bright, she stands straight and smiles for no apparent reason. We both have money in the bank, but that doesn't make us remotely the same. Our common ground has room for a pinky toe and no more.

But we're also both women, and I know that counts for more than a foot's smallest digit. And more than just having similar physiology. Rich or not, there are similarities in our worries, in our plight. There might have been real-life *Bobs* in her life, just like there have been in mine. No one deserves a Bob.

She waits for me to say something without the least sign of impatience. She's so damn sweet and polite.

"There's a guy who works there, across the street. His name is Wolf. He's a real good person. You can tell him I sent you."

She nods.

"Ok then. Have a nice life."

I grab my keys and pull off the ones for the shop, making it final. Standing on the wrong side of the counter, I am now just another medium-height, medium-brown-haired rude-ass customer.

Stepping out, I put my nose to the breeze, the sweetness of freedom floating about like the scent of freshly blossoming lilacs on a spring day. A small knot of excitement sits in my stomach as I hop a bus that will take me to the next neighbourhood over.

I pull out the soup-stained piece of paper. On it is an address. Once close enough, I get off and search the backstreets for the mystery house I've yet to see with my real, woken eyes. A few zigzags down some handsome blocks and I find it, a big "for sale" sign planted in its front yard with the words "Open House" taped across it. It's a huge, white monstrosity of a house with a landscaped front yard, a number of pillars, bay windows, and an intricate, flowery cornice lining the roof's edge. I follow the cobblestone walkway up to the door.

"This is going to be my house," I say to myself, ringing the doorbell. A slight unease quivers in my blood, making my body buzz. I wonder what sort of memories I implanted in this man's mind, and if I am walking straight into the spider's web.

The door opens and a chill runs up my spine. At first, Bob looks surprised, almost  frightened, but he quickly relaxes, and smiles.

"Hello," he says, stroking the head of a fluffy, black-and-white tabby cradled tightly in his oversized arms. I notice a bandage wrapped around his right bicep: the lion's mark.

The cat, which looks a lot like the one that used to wait for me and its daily jerky, looks annoyed at the heavy petting. It wriggles free just as Bob bends down to set it to the ground. If only he had let me go so smoothly. I watch the cat strut its blob of fur towards the wall, rub its side at the corner, meow, and run off.

"Come on in," Bob says, moving out of the way.

"Thank you, Sir." I stand tall and straighten my shirt, which does not show any cleavage. If I owned a turtleneck, I'd have worn it. His eyes drop to my chest nonetheless, his fingers twitching by his sides. I regret letting him feel my boobs. Even in dreamworld, my body's not a negotiating asset. But, most importantly, he proved himself very unworthy. I pray he keeps his hands to himself. I cut to the chase.

"I'm ready to buy the house."

"You haven't even visited yet."

"Uh, yes, of course. It's just so beautiful on the outside, I know I'll love it."

Bob shows me around. Everything is as I had dreamed—the pool, the glass wall, the balcony; even the bedroom upstairs, which I make a point to only poke my head in, and which he himself introduces with a hesitant strain in his voice.

He shows me the inspection report. Everything is tip top, the house built just a few years ago. He's selling without an agent. A better price for me, he says. Not that I care. I'm rich.

"So this money you came into, it's an inheritance?"

"No, insurance money."

He nods and shrugs.

"Hey, money's money. It's all the same to me."

I am the first to visit, so I get dibs. I call the bank on the spot, and they confirm that the transfer can be done today. Bob and I arrange to meet there later and get the deed signed over with a notary. We shake hands, and he pulls out a pen. It's the same pen. I shudder as he hands it to me.

Signing my name on the new, clean promise to purchase, I feel him standing close. Too close. His cologne reeks, teasing a lump of nausea up my throat. I hand him the pen with trembling hands. He looks down at it, turning it in his fingers. Frowning, he taps it in his palm a few times and looks at me, clearly confused. I eye the door, ready to dart for it if he were to suddenly turn on me. But instead he bends over the papers, leaving a cloud of perfume behind. The man stinks. I imagine him rubbing his body all over with the would-be scratch-and-sniff of a fashion magazine. The mental picture makes me chuckle, and I relax. It's done.

The house is mine as of next week, since Bob is leaving for San Francisco. His sister Frances has fallen ill from severe salmonella, and he needs to be with her.

Everything is moving much faster than I expected, and by the time May's first shift is done, I've bought a house. I peek in as I walk by. She's smiling, the imp.

I step into my apartment and look around. Damn place. I wouldn't wish it on anyone, magical pills or not.

The pink pills.

I double check the jar. It's empty, the last one knocking me out last night. With Eveleen's moaning and all the clacks, clicks, wails and ticks, I'm sure to get no sleep here. Just a few more nights before I can burying my nose into my new, quiet, rich-lady house. Just a few nights. I step out onto my balcony and look down at the Spin Factory. I sigh, my lips flapping loudly.

"Just keep it cold, Edie," I say, closing the doors behind me.

# ELEVEN

"You really don't mind? I don't want to be a burden."

"It's all good, Edie. My couch is your couch," Wolf says, counting up his cash on the counter.

"You're angry with me, aren't you?"

"No, no. It's all good. People are complex. I respect you, Edie. You're a bit unpredictable, but that's fine. I got your back."

"So, friends?"

"Friends?" He looks up, pleased, and goes back to thumbing his bills. "Sure."

By the time he's done all the after-closing-time stuff, it's well past 9 p.m.

"Wow, you really take this seriously."

It takes a second for Wolf to realize what I'm talking about.

"Closing shop? Why wouldn't I? It's mine. I love it. I take care of it."

"This shop is yours?"

"Yep."

I step out onto the moonlit sidewalk and let him lock the door from the outside.

"Where do you live?" I ask him.

"A fifteen minute walk that way." He points to downtown with his chin, his hands still busy with the lock. "Is that ok?"

"Ya, of course. Legs," I say, pointing at my legs. He acknowledges their existence with a nod.

"Are you hungry? There's a good take-out on the way."

We eat as we walk, mostly in silence. The night feels strange. Everything is different in the dark. The streets take on a different life, the trees a different shape, the air a different scent. Movement and sound have a bewitching quality; a charm I learned to distrust.

It's been a long while since I turned my back on nightlife. Intoxication, shifty encounters and their sneaky enchantment were traded for a safe and predictable routine—one I think about longingly now, as I stand on skewed and slippery ground.

We arrive at Wolf's one-bedroom bachelor apartment. His place is tiny. There are only a few things inside. He probably couldn't fit more even if he wanted to. The potential is maxed out at a couch and a bed, a small table and a smaller coffee table. There's also a tiny TV, with a stereo beneath it. A few plants burst through macramé hangers. A computer hides in a corner. A guitar sits in another.

"You play?"

"Um, ya. Just for fun." He plops off his shoes by the door. I do the same and hang my sweater on the coat rack.

"So, this is my place." He displays the surroundings with his hand, from left to right, finishing with the couch. "Your temporary bed."

"No walls, huh? Just like my place."

Wolf makes his way behind the small kitchen counter and pours two glasses of water. He comes back with both and hands one to me.

"Is that a problem?"

"No." I take the glass and sit down.

"Great. Give me a minute?"

"Of course."

Wolf fiddles around with stuff, and I do my best to ignore him, not wanting to invade his space any further. The water tastes good and I focus on that, taking little sips. I jiggle it and twirl it in the glass, looking up briefly every so often. Wolf is tidying the kitchen. My water is clear but there's a black speck in it. I pick it out by pushing it up against the side. Wolf is picking up clothes from the floor. I tip my glass to my lips and try to see how steep I can lean it before the water hits my mouth and goes up my nose. Wolf is standing in front of me, his arms decked with linen.

"If I may," he says.

I wipe my face with my sleeve, put the glass down and stand up. We spread out the sheets and the blanket together, and he leaves for the bathroom. Quickly, I take my pants off and unsling my bra, pulling it out through my shirt's sleeve hole, and slip under the bedding before Wolf comes back. I'm not a prude, but I don't trust Wolf more than I do any man, or woman, for that matter. There will be no tempting of the devil. Especially the day after Bob.

"This window faces east, right?" I ask when I hear him step out.

"Yes, I think."

"Could we leave the blinds open?"

"Sure."

The streetlights keep the apartment dimly lit. Wolf climbs into his own bed in his boxer shorts, his bedsprings creaking loudly as he bounces his way into place. He seems happy with his lot. He has his own shop, but other than that he doesn't seem to have much. He doesn't even have a good bed. Even I have a good bed. It's not a frivolity. You don't need to be rich to have a good bed. Why doesn't he have a good bed? He can't be poor. He owns his shop. He loves his job. Maybe loving your job is really what it means to be wealthy, and not the things you have. Or is loving your job a luxury? Can you have luxury in your life, and still be poor?

"Wolf?" I ask from across the coffee table.

"Yup?"

"Are you poor?"

He doesn't answer right away.

"I don't think so."

"Oh." I think for a second. "I am. I mean, I was." I turn onto my side away from him, my face an inch from the couch's back, and pull the sheet up over my shoulder.

"I was," I say again, the words lost in the softness of my own breath.

Not having my pills makes me a little anxious, but it's effortlessly calm and quiet here. I might actually have a regular night's sleep, without any drama, any reality manipulation. Wolf tosses in his squeaky bed, and then silence. I'm out as soon as my top lashes meet their bottom half.

The dream I find myself in is bright and vivid; I'm as lucid as I've been every night for the past week.

I'm standing in a prison common room. The place is packed. There's dancing, streamers, and strobe lights. People shout to be heard, "Can't you Hear me Knocking" by The Rolling Stones blasting from invisible speakers.

The veil of consciousness distancing me from my sleeping body is quite thin, or my hearing particularly acute, because I can hear Wolf snoring, piercing through the hullabaloo in my head, just like with Eveleen's voice when I slept at building fifty-one. The rolling of Wolf's breath idles like a motorcycle, circling outside the prison room. I follow the sound, exiting the room easily, the door unlocked.

On the other side of the wall is a dining room. I'm interrupting dinner, it seems. A family of seven sits at a table, forks in hand. Their eyes narrow at the sight of me. I walk through, dirtying their carpet with my muddy boots, and follow Wolf's snore all the way to another door. It opens onto a field. Not a blade of grass grows from the ground, the earth compact and dry, small clouds of dust keeping low as they pass like blanket of curling mist above the sea.

Wolf is sitting on a tree stump, some fifty feet away. His snore has dissipated, making way for words. He barely moves his lips but I hear him speaking clearly.

"I don't want to," he says. "Let me just stay here. Please." He repeats these words as he gets up and walks out towards what I see now is a cliff's edge. He heads straight for it.

I want to yell out to him, but, lacking the heart to put the effort, I don't. My eyes watch his form slip from view, right off the cliff.

"Shit. Why the hell would he do that?" I run to the edge and look down. The cliff is so high. A queazy knot grabs me in the stomach and forces my feet back, though I keep my eyes over the lip of the drop-off. Wolf's shape becomes smaller and smaller as he plummets.

"He'll be fine. People fall in dreams all the time," I reassure myself, though pin-pricking doubt coats my words.

Didn't real-life Bob end up with a bite wound because of me? What if my presence causes Wolf to really splatter once he hits the ground?

If he had wings, he could fly right back up, I think to myself. Squinting my eyes, I concentrate, picturing wings on his back, that I might manifest them. But nothing happens, and Wolf falls. It's done. He's gone.

A weighty blanket of regret weighs over my shoulders. My heart thuds slow, sad thumps. Nothing left but to wake and find him lifeless. Life will go on, and Wolf will remain an unsullied memory of a good friend. We will never be given the chance to mess it up.

Just before I turn away, I see a form: Wolf, out on the horizon, flying like a fucking eagle.

The eastern sun heats my exposed shoulder. I push myself to a sitting position, drinking my fill of its warmth while remembering where I am and why I'm here. Wolf is already up, sipping a steaming coffee at his little mustard-yellow table. Another mug is set across from him.

"Good morning," he says, hardly looking away from his phone. "Sorry, just catching up on my social media."

"Really?" I slip on my jeans and join him. For some reason I have a hard time imagining him as a virtual socialite.

"You know, for the store. I post pics of the record sleeves, to connect with music lovers, and also to attract some clients."

The coffee is too hot to drink.

"You have some milk?"

"Yes, help yourself."

His fridge is full of colourful vegetables, jars of who-knows-what jams, and smoothie bottles. I grab the soy milk.

"This all you got?"

"'Fraid so. I haven't drunk booby milk in ages."

"Booby milk?"

"Animal milk comes from boobs, Edie."

I grin as I pour the stuff in my mug until my coffee is golden. It does the trick.

"Coffee's good, thank you."

"Did you sleep all right?"

"Perfectly. Thank you so much."

"I slept really good, too. I mean, there's this recurring nightmare I've been having. I dream that I walk straight off a cliff and just fall, and fall, like, forever. Of course I wake up just as I hit the ground, but it's a long way down and it's scary. Well, last night, I grew wings. Wings! And I flew, Edie! Just like you did!"

I think for a second, and remember I had told him about it in a dream, just before making out with him on his store counter.

"How do you know I flew?"

"Because you told me?"

"When?"

"When?" Wolfs scans the table like it was a map to his memories. "I don't remember. But we were at the Spin."

I take another sip of coffee.

"Have we ever kissed?"

He looks up, his cheeks pink. "Ha ha. Not that I'm aware of. Not in real life. I mean, I've had a few dreams. One in particular would probably make you blush."

My coffee mug becomes my point of focus, keeping my eyes away from Wolf's while I think. I'm relieved, but also worried. All arrows point to the same conclusion. I've been messing with Wolf's dreams. Bob's dreams. *Eveleen's* dreams. I look up and grin.

"Hey, it happens to everyone." But that's absurd. This does not happen to everyone. Not like this.

Toasts pop. Wolf serves them with almond butter, and freshly squeezed orange juice. Best breakfast I've had in years. So simple, yet delicious and real.

"You want to come back tonight?" Wolf asks after downing his juice.

"Now that you've confessed dreaming about me? I don't think so!"

"Really? Who cares. I'm the same, cold acquaintance. Couldn't care less. Go sleep in your crazy-house without your *sleeping supplements*, then."

He had a point.

"Wolf?"

"Yes?"

"Can I sleep on your couch tonight?"

"Yes." He laughs and shakes his head.


Back at building fifty-one, I receive a call about the house. As it turns out, there's only one more night and I can move in. One night and I'm free.

The poker-faced landlady comes by. She doesn't give a flying hoot that I'm leaving, she says. She has bigger fish to fry than run after sensitive girlies who can't deal with life in the city. Girls like me are soft. Life hasn't hardened us enough yet. Too much coddling from Mommy, she says. We expect the world to nurture and baby us the same way our mommies did. She didn't know my mother, apparently.

Two months rent was all it took for her to quit her ranting.

The last hours of daylight are spent running around for boxes. There's not much to pack, the plants being the most awkward to transport. Wolf said he'd help me, which is a kind thing to do, and hence made me hesitate to accept. It's by habit that I always refuse, but in this case it's also an act of self-preservation. He's already letting me sleep on his couch. Generosity is not inexhaustible; at some point, he's going to want something from me.

The last of the boxes are taped up.

"We'd better get out of here," I tell Wolf.

"Why?"

"Well, you're going to be tired for work tomorrow. Also, this is around the time I usually hit the sack. I'm a creature of habit."

"This time, huh? So when does the zoo wake up?"

"Really soon."

Wolf's face lights up.

"Oh, I wanna hear."

"Really, Wolf, I just want to go crash now. Can we?"

He sits down on the edge of the bare mattress.

"Oh, man!" He says, bouncing a little. "Now, this is a bed!"

I stay on my feet, tapping my foot, my arms crossed. But he doesn't budge. And then it starts. As usual, Eveleen is first. Wolf's head snaps up at me, his eyes wide with childlike excitement, a big grin on his face. He soon realizes Eveleen means business.

"Oh." He travels somewhere in his mind as he listens. But then there are the sewing machines, the tap dancing, and something new. Arpeggios. Someone has reserved this time for singing practice. Wolf looks up again and nods, finally understanding my predicament.

"This is fucking mental!"

"Wait," I tell him. And the baby starts wailing. Poor baby. "Heard enough?"

"Hell, ya."

# TWELVE

We grab some food on the way to Wolf's and eat in front of his tiny TV, watching an obscure fifties movie.

"It's too much," I say.

"What is?"

"The acting. Everything is such a big deal. The girl, she's so ... emotional."

"You don't like that."

"Well, it's just so fake. The guy's not very believable either. Have you ever spoken that way in real life? 'Do not fear, I will save you, my dear!'"

He shrugs, suggesting that perhaps he has.

"I'm not surprised," I say.

"How so?"

"You're organized, dedicated. You give things your all. Or so it seems. I could see you jumping in front of a train for your lady-love."

"You think too highly of me."

"Not too much, don't worry. You're just different. From me, anyway. And most people who look out for number one."

"Ah, I look out for number one, too. Like now. I'm going to eat this last pickle, without offering it to you first." He winks at me, and I smile, just to be nice. The iciness that coated our pseudo-acquaintanceship is most obviously melted. Even though I know it was never cold to begin with, it's important for me to believe it was, and still is. I know what I need. Closeness isn't it. And so I run, mentally, catching the thawed droplets before they hit the ground and make warmth final.

The sheets that were used the night before are laid back out on the couch, the pillow tossed at the end. We go through the same motions, except that I lie awake for a short while before falling. There's no noise to prevent my fall, only nerves. Even without the pills, I'm still lucid dreaming, and anything my mind can conceive, consciously or not, can mess with life on the outside, whether I want to or not.

In the field again, the one with the cliff, Wolf sits on the same stump, his bare back turned to me. He's working on something. His arm moves back and forth in front of him. His beige work-pants and large rubber boots are speckled with wood shavings. A fine layer of sawdust covers his skin, clinging to his sweat.

"Wolf." I approach him.

He doesn't turn around.

"Wolf," I repeat, louder. He turns, sees me, and goes right back to work.

"I need to get this done … on time," he says through grunts of effort. "It needs to be good."

It's not clear whether Wolf is in my dream, or I am in his. It's both, perhaps. His glassy gaze clearly indicates that, whatever the case, he is not lucid as I am.

"What are you making?" I ask him.

"A chair."

"For who?"

"For her."

Shit. He's already making me imaginary gifts. Maybe this would be a good place to get through to him. To let him know that we are not going to happen. I sit on the ground beside him amidst the cream-coloured wood curls, wondering how I could possibly wake him up. Not as in back in the apartment, but as in here, in the field. Make him lucid, like me.

"Wolf," I say, putting my hand on his arm. "Stop for a minute."

He does, and looks at me with dreamy eyes.

"Look at your hands." He does as I say. "Now, count your fingers."

"One, two, three ... I have four thumbs."

"That's not normal, right?"

"That's weird."

"You're dreaming, Wolf."

He looks confused.

"Stay calm, ok? You're dreaming. Look."

My hands held up before him, I move a finger from one hand towards the palm of my other hand until it touches it. Then I push it right through to the other side.

"Stay calm," I tell him again, "or you'll wake up."

He nods at my hands and looks at me. There's a glimmer of awareness there.

"Wow."

"I know." I smile. He's awake.

Looking around, he lets his surroundings sink in.

"What am I wearing?" He chuckles. Then there's the chair. "I'm making that chair for my wife."

"Your what?"

"My ex-wife. She left me. She didn't love me anymore. I guess it's a good reason to leave someone. She's out there somewhere, travelling, having fun."

I feel stupid for thinking the chair was for me. But this is good news. He still loves his ex-wife. I can stop worrying.

"Wolf, you wanna fly?"

He smiles, letting his nostalgia settle back into that place where it lives, but doesn't quite thrive, and smiles. "Hell, ya."

He pulls off his rubber boots and shakes his pants clean. We get up and dart into a run. It's not as fast as I'd want, the laws of sleep always having the upper hand over my legs, but we run fast enough to give us a bit of momentum to outrun our fear as we dive into the open sky at the edge of the world.

I've flown once before. It was wonderful, and scary too. But this is different. We fly out, and up, suspended by only a warm breeze, and, like vultures or hawks, we soar. The world below is distant, so miniature it's practically non-existent. Wolf laughs and throws himself forward in a tumble, and then extends his arms and legs, his clothes bulging like webbing.

"You look like a squirrel!" I yell at him.

"What?"

He dives down and I dive down after him. We speed towards a cloud. I'm racing him, and, though I don't say so, I can tell he knows by the smirk on his face. We pierce through, cold droplets speckling our faces, the air around us foggy and white. I can see nothing, and soon feel disoriented and dizzy. Wolf is gone.

I feel a tug at my leg. I'm on the ground, in a desert. The ground is warm, the sun bright. Cacti are scattered sporadically around me, their tall bodies and crooked arms creating ghostly shadows across the red earth. I feel the tug again and look. There's no one there. It tugs again, and, finally, I open my eyes to the darkness of the bachelor apartment. His face faintly illuminated by the light coming through the window, Wolf is at the foot of the couch, tapping my ankle gently.

"What are you doing?" I ask in a scraggly voice.

"Edie, that was amazing."

"I know."

He crawls around the front and stares at me wide-eyed.

"I feel high." He caresses my hair down my face.

I freeze. "What are you doing, Wolf."

"Edie, thank you."

"You're welcome."

He puts his hand back in his lap.

Half of my body is still dreaming, the other half is awake, trying to recall why I don't want a romantic relationship. I don't trust men, that's why. I just want to go back to my magical dream. Because that's what it was. Sharing it with Wolf was magic.

"Wolf, what about your wife?"

"She's gone, Edie."

Wolf hesitates, then strokes my hair again. His hand is warm as the sand in the desert. My heart pounds syncopated rhythms against my ribs, urging me to just let it explode, and make a mess in my chest. If only I was still sleeping. Then, perhaps, I could indulge again. What if I am still sleeping? And what difference does it make, when the lines between sleep and wakefulness are so blurred? When fantasies can't stay confined to their plane of existence anymore, travelling impartially from one to the other? It doesn't make a difference. Therefore these feelings are better left alone, tightly wound and tossed, ignored as a hankering that will go away if I just don't feed it.

Wolf pulls his hand back again and smiles. He understands.

"Wait." I frown, and lock eyes with him for a while. And then I nod. He comes closer, looking up at me as if to make sure. I say nothing. Panic digs its claws into my stomach as he moves in for a kiss, and my heart, and my body, betrays every objection my reasoning mind has. Like a sappy fifties actress, I pull him in.

Off the couch and onto the carpeted floor, clothes are torn off. With our hankering hands, our watering mouths, everything is velvet, pudding, chocolate, silk. Desire is exposed, unashamed. Embraced, and consumed. For the next few hours of darkness, the world we are in is neither here nor there. A third dimension of ecstasy. We discover its sacred valleys and otherworldly crests with the undying stamina of wolves and dreamers.

When the sun rises, it does not land on me. Its rays fall on the empty couch. I look at its golden light from Wolf's bed, and regret that I'm not waking to its caresses, preferring those to anyone else's.

The lustre's gone.

My clothes too far to reach, I walk out to them with the whole bedsheet wrapped around me, leaving Wolf exposed.

"Sorry," I tell him, unable to stop grinning.

"That's all right. I'll cover up with my blinding joy."

I stop in my tracks, a pinch in my heart, then bend down to pick up my stuff. A twisted length of the white linen drags behind me as I head for the bathroom. Halfway there, I stop again.

"Listen, Wolf…"

"Don't worry, Edie. It's ok. I'm a friend. And I can go back to being just that. I'd understand. You can think about it, if you want."

"I don't really want to think about it." I look away. "I just don't want … this."

The silence is my cue to get changed and get out.

My moral compass is fucked. I lost control with Wolf because of that dream. It was too comfortable. Too magical. And then, he was being too nice. Too charming. Of course, I had to tell him we couldn't be together. Because we all know how these things end.

# THIRTEEN

The door buzzer rings. It must be the moving guys. I only need a small truck, for the bed. Otherwise I could have fit everything in the back of a family van. Moving guy number two slides to the middle and lets me have the window seat, so as to not sandwich me between him and moving guy number one. I find this particularly sweet, and so I suppose number two wants a tip.

It takes longer to drive to the new house than to unload my things. The movers take turns shaking my hand and leave without the pause that would indicate that they expect a tip. I feel a bit like a shmuck for assuming they would. To make up for it, I call out to them just before they climb back into their truck.

"Thank you!" I wave, smiling like an idiot.

There's something a bit eerie about the new place, having dreamt about it first before ever setting my real eyes on it. I say real eyes, as if my dream vision isn't true, or reliable. Maybe it isn't. But neither is my waking life then. Either they are both valid, or both questionable. The ambiguity is hard to accept.

Light pours in through the windows and fills the large, empty space, exposing its cold colours. The walls are a dark blue-grey, accentuated by the distressed, light-grey hardwood floors. My plants all set down by the entrance, I bring a few into the living room, and already the place feels more like home. Unpacking is an uneventful chore. I know exactly what is in each of those boxes. There is no element of surprise. They are not gifts to open, but only my shit, moved from one place to the other, which in no way excites me. I decide to leave it for later.

Instead I unlatch the glass doors to the back porch and step outside. Only slightly shaded by the cedars fencing the yard, the area is bright and big enough to install a greenhouse. A few minutes are given to the courageous act of dreaming.

It all feels unreal, like I just might wake up at any given moment. As if a fragile thread is tying me down, and I could sneeze, and it would break, and I would float away, far into the realms of insanity. Despite this, I feel happy.

And something I keep forgetting comes back to me: I'm rich. So I do something different. I shop. Hard.

Sitting in the middle of the floor in a beam of sunlight, I spend the next hours on my phone, ordering furniture, clothes, electronics, gardening equipment, seeds, bulbs, and dirt. I even order my groceries online. What a glorious time we live in. Thanks to these cyber retailers and the many delivery services that cater to them, we can stay inside our homes and never see anyone if we don't want to. Easily. This might be the best realization to ever dawn on me.

The room I choose as my sleeping quarters is on the top floor, at the opposite corner from the room where Bob touched my boobs. Unfortunately, I don't think I'm about to forget that. My new sleeping kingdom has both an east- and a south-facing window, the latter with a view of the yard. The room itself is nice and big, easily fitting four queen-size beds and enough floor space left to dance with Phil Collins should the urge arise. It has a door that opens and closes, and walls that will not breathe of the lust of strangers.

Wooden chopsticks sticking out from between my fingers and my mouth full of Chinese take-out, I bring my few boxes from the entrance and up the half-stairs to the main room. I look around for something to cut through the packing tape with, and decide to jab it with my single-pronged utensil. After the kitchen shit, clothes, and records, I finally poke my way through to the toiletries. Leaving the opened boxes on the floor, I pull out my toothbrush, toothpaste and pyjamas.

My bedroom windows are open and fresh night air blows through, bringing with it only a few nocturnal animal sounds. No tap dancing, no sewing machines, no babies, no moaning. Dreamworld comes without a hitch.

I'm standing naked in the middle of my dark bedroom. Outside, rain falls steadily, the million pitter patters creating a soothing white noise, broken only by crashes of lightning which illuminate my surroundings at every strike. I walk out of my room, suddenly clothed, which is good because my house is full of people. The music is loud out here. A DJ is set up on the kitchen counter, before which a crowd is dancing, their raised arms flashing rhythmically under the strobes. As there is still no furniture, people are for the most part standing.

Some sit on the floor. Through the patio window I see people in the yard, and the pool. Lightning throws a fork across the clouds and lights up the sky.

"There are people in the pool," I mutter to myself. I want to warn them, but the door is jammed. Thunder claps. Panic creeps in. I wiggle the handle, turn the latch back and forth, pull and push the door into a furious rattle. I yell, as loudly as I can, banging my fists against the glass. They don't turn.

Another spear of light is thrown down, and, in a mere parenthesis of time, makes brilliant the ragged shapes of the fencing cedars, the tops of neighbouring houses, the silhouettes of the bodies down in the grass, and the faces, howling with laughter, of those in the pool, just before it strikes the water like an angry scorpion. At first I see red ghosts, then bright skeletal features, mouths agape and eyeless sockets, and, an instant later, they are gone. The scream that shot from me did nothing to prevent it. My pool is dark with ash.

The party behind me doesn't ease. Shoving my way down the stairs, I hurry to the rec room and through to the back yard. People stand around the pool in the drizzling rain, drinking and chatting, oblivious to the disappearance of a whole crowd that was there minutes before. Only a dark film is left covering the water. I grab the first guy beside me and shake him.

"What the hell is wrong with you?"

"Edie, life is peachy! Have a drink," he slurs, and shoves a bottle in my hand. I pass it to the next person over, and go to the edge of the pool.

Kneeling by the water, I plunge my hands in deep and swoosh them around. The water under the film is also dark, and I can't see into it. But there are lumps, what feels like dozens of them, brushing up against my arms. I trap some in my cupped palms and pull them out.

Whatever colours the water also stains my skin black, like a dip-dyed candle, from elbows to fingertips. I bring the back of my hand to my nose. It only smells like me. Unfurling a finger at a time, my black hands reveal a bunch of teeth in each palm. Shivers run up my body. This dream has taken a bad turn. It's time to wake myself up.

No, not yet. What if morning comes and reveals a pool full of charred flesh and teeth? This mess has to be dealt with.

I don't know how to drain a pool. But this is a dream. For a second I doubt, count my fingers, and continue ahead with the dreamworld play-dough I can shape to my will.

"The drain is here," I decide, and open a small shed.

I slap my hand around the inside of the wall, looking for a light switch. I flick it, but it stays dark.

"Right."

There is just enough glow from the house to see the shape of a few tanks and the pipes connected to them. Not too worried about whether it is the right thing to do, I grab a lever sticking out from one of the tanks and push it upwards. A big sucking noise comes from outside, like a bathtub emptying itself. It seems exaggerated, yet exactly what I expect to hear. By the time I step out, the water is already gone, but the teeth remain. There must be millions of them.

I run into the rec room and make a beeline for the mini bar, to the cupboard beneath the sink, because that is where garbage bags live. Though I remember I haven't yet bought any of the junk that goes beneath a sink, I also know I haven't bought beer, nor invited any of these people. This is a dream.

"Big black garbage bags, please," I say before opening the door, seeing a box clearly in my mind's eye. And there it is, its flap open with a bag ready to be plucked. "Fucking brilliant!" I run back out and hand bags to a few people. "Help me bag these teeth!"

We climb down the pool's steel ladder, hopping to the bottom, all three of us slipping and falling on the tiny enamel nugget. It takes many attempts, slipping over and over again, catching ourselves with our hands or falling on our butts, before finally finding a secure footing on the pool lining.

Scooping the teeth with our arms, we fill six large bags, then haul them up onto the edge and shove them into the tiny shed, beside the tanks. One of the guys, the one who assured me that life is peachy, puts his arm around my shoulders and says, "Come, let's go have a drink." And we do.

We dance, sweat, laugh, and drink until we can't speak straight. And I forget all about the dead pool people and their millions of teeth.

My phone rings. My hand sweeps the floor beside my bed.

"Yeeesss?" My voice sounds like I swallowed a pack of nails, its abrasiveness giving me an instant headache. "Oh, you're outside now? Ok, I'm coming."

My eyelids open, and the morning light stabs me in the retinas, amplifying the pounding at my temples. Stumbling into some clothes, I stagger down to the front door.

"Hello, we have a delivery for Eddie?" He eyes me strangely. I look myself over, to my right arm, to my left. They are stained black. I decide to ignore the weirdness of it completely. I'm rich and I can be as goddamn eccentric as I please.

"That's *Edie*, and it's me. Come on in."

Three guys start unloading the truck of furniture. Leading them first into the open living room, I block their way at the threshold. The floor is littered with bottles and cans, ashtrays, clothing and shoes. I scratch my sore head.

The men place the furniture where I show them, avoiding any trash I haven't kicked out of the way first, and head back out. An hour later my floor is completely foot-swept and decked with velvet couches, exotic wood tables, ornate Victorian chairs, commodes, buffets, and shit I don't know the name to that just looked real good in the pictures.

Before I have time to brush my teeth and wash the hangover off my face, the doorbell rings. Another delivery truck, with appliances. Fridge, stove, dishwasher, washer and dryer. My laundromat days are over. After that truck comes yet another, this time with all sorts of useless knick-knacks, but also the most practical stuff, like plates, cutlery, chandeliers, and crystal turtles. Over the course of the day, my house is stocked with everything from pushpins to pickled baby fucking onions. I am rich, goddamn it. And my house is brimming with gorgeous shit.

The deliveries are done. The front entrance is blocked with a mountain of empty boxes and plastic wrappings. Showered and renewed, I finally lay a record on my new turntable just as the sun decides to spread its reddish blanket across the sky. Stan Getz flows from all corners of the room like unctuous waves of honey into my ears. I strut to my shiny new monster-of-a-fridge, and hum with delight at all the colourful food bursting from its shelves.

"I have so much food." I smile as I tap it all with my index finger, taking my time choosing what to eat. The ingredients all laid out on the marble-top island, I am Julia fucking Child. The food ends up being fantastic too, even if only because of the variety of vegetables I put in and the plenitude of spices at my disposal.

After my pretty damn good meal, I step out onto the balcony. My pool has no water in it.

"Oh shit, that's right." Distracted by the arrival of all the stuff I ever wanted, I forgot that disaster. The details of my dream trickle back in, as does my lingering hangover headache.

But I didn't really drink, I think to myself. I look over at the yard below, a space that almost feels like it belongs in another world, and wonder what other mess has successfully crossed the invisible border.

In the shed, big black garbage bags are tucked into the corners behind the tanks. With shaking, stained fingers I untie one of them. It is filled with teeth. Incisors, canines, and molars. Choppers. Pearly whites. Chicklets. My back against the rough hemlock wood of the shed wall, I slide down inch by inch and sit on the ground. Panic. Hyperventilation. A build-up of tears. *Shit shit shit shit shit*, and so forth. A handful of teeth shoved in my pocket, I tie the bag shut and run inside.

"Elvira," I call out. I called my smart TV assistant Elvira, hoping I'd be talking to the internet under funnier circumstances. "Give me the news."

"Hello, EE-DEE. It would be my pleasure."

A list drops down and I choose the local news, scrolling through with my remote. Nothing on the disappearance of a few dozen people. Nor a few hundred people. Maybe it's too soon.

"I should have called the cops the minute those numb-nuts were barbecued," I say to myself, wondering if phones work in the sleep world, or if they become unreliable, like clocks, light switches, and common sense.

Were the numb-nuts in question real people? Now that I am meddling with their subconscious as much as they are with mine, individualistic dream experience is obsolete. It's a shared enterprise, between me and the world. How could I ever differentiate between a person who has a real mirror-self on the other side, and one that doesn't? How can I tell if they are only a figment of my imagination? What about when you dream about two people in one? When uncle George is also Simon Le Bon from Duran Duran? If I were to stab George-Simon, would they both die?

It's like I'm playing a game of battleship, poking at empty spaces, never knowing if the boats will match on both sides. I have no anchorage, and I'm always going about it half-blind. The waters are choppy and it's making me seasick.

My fingers flick the nuggets around in my pocket, making soft clicking sounds.

Going to the authorities, or a forensic dentist who might tell on me, smells like trouble. I didn't ask the lightning to fry the buggers. Still, it couldn't possibly turn out good if we found out these were the teeth of two dozen young adults from the Green Square, alive and kicking just a day ago, busy with their usual shopping, brunching, and getting jobs they don't need.

If I do it in my sleep, can I count on the results?

At this point I don't know why, but I still put my faith in my waking life being the most valid reality. Maybe it's just reassuring. One of them has to be more real, no? How could I ever fully trust the intangible over the material? Despite this, I decide to try my luck identifying the teeth in my dreamworld first. Though the risk might be just as great, with all its unpredictability, at least the dream I can manipulate.

# FOURTEEN

When night fully drops, my eyelids follow, and I dive into my mind, into a world that has become foreign and fickle.

Standing in a bookstore, still as a display, I'm facing a dirty man draped in torn, threadbare clothes. He's going to mug me, I'm almost sure, because in my pockets I have all my money. Like eight hundred dollars or something. Which is less than in waking life, but right now, this is my reality. Eight hundred dollars is the total of my riches. And, in a dream, when you have that kind of money on you and a beggar stares you down, you know that they know it's there. There are many people around, and mugging me would be stupid, maybe even impossible. He takes a step closer, his smell as assaulting as a slap in the face.

"Frank?" I say, recognizing him from what feels like a previous life.

"If you give me your eight hundred, I can give you even more." He flashes an ATM receipt to prove that he has shitloads of cash in the bank. "Follow me."

For some reason, I do. But just before stepping outside, I flick my wrist, which is still stained from the pool's ashes, and all the people crowding the store follow me out. Just a few picks and shovels short of being an angry mob, we make our way down a city street and up to an ATM machine. I give the man three hundred only. Without a word of protest, he deposits it, and the machine responds by spewing out bills like a broken copy machine from an eighties comedy.

"I've never seen so much money in my life," I say.

Frank collects his three hundred from the pile, and I shove as much as I can in my pockets, in my shoes, up my sleeves, in my bra. Money pokes out of every nook like hay from a scarecrow. Frank stands before me, quietly assessing my loot. He still wants to mug me, that much is clear, but I'm surrounded by onlookers, so he leaves. When I turn, the scene has changed. Everyone is gone, the city is gone, I'm standing on dirt ground. I'm by the cliff where Wolf and I flew.

I double check my hands to make sure I'm still dreaming, and, though dyed black, they are perfectly deformed. That's good enough for me.

"Ok. Let's get to it."

My money, having neatly rolled itself into tight wads all on its own, weighs down my pockets so much I have to hold on to my waistband to keep my pants up. I flag a cab with my free hand.

"To the forensic dentist's office, please," I tell him. "And step on it." I've always wanted to say that.

We speed forward, clouds of dust swelling behind us. Through the woods that line the field, we swerve to avoid trees at a speed that will either make me puke or die. We don't die, and I hold my stomach down as the car jets out of the forest and onto the sandy grounds of a vast, rust-coloured desert. Two hundred metres away, a cabin. The driver slams on the brakes, sending my face into the back of the passenger seat.

"Give me your money!" he shouts.

I know by this he means all my money. So I guess this is how it goes. You get a little, and suddenly everybody wants their share. Even if they have to beat it out of you. I throw a nickel at him and dash out, running to get to the little lone building where the cowboy dentist lives. Of course, my legs feel like they are stuck in mud. My heart thumps wildly, knowing the taxi driver is behind me.

"I'm dreaming, I'm dreaming!" I shout, urgently reminding myself. A grip on the door handle, I turn back to look: the driver and his taxi are gone. A hitched breath staggering its way in, I force myself to exhale slowly before entering.

The place looks like a regular doctor's office, though it smells of roast chicken. A man in white scrubs shows up and shakes my hand. He's my guy. I follow him down a well-lit corridor and into an operating room. Little glass jars full of organs line the wall. One seems to contain a small but fully developed puppy.

"I need you to identify some teeth," I tell him as I empty my pockets on a stainless steel table. Teeth and rolls of cash mixed with paperclips and a few gum balls. He plucks from the pile and heads over to a microscope. A tooth appears on his computer screen and, beside it, images flash at a fantastic speed as possible matches are filtered through. I decide to eat one of the gum balls while I wait. Watermelon.

"These fourteen teeth belong to these fourteen people," he informs me.

I leave the clinic with the only wad of cash left. The tiny list of names folded in my pocket cost me almost everything I had.

"Time to wake up!" I clap my hands in a show of conclusiveness, with no one to convince but myself. I'm tired of sleeping. Pinching my inner arm, fake scaring myself, holding my breath, squeezing my eyes real tight and opening them again. Nothing works. I'm a bit worried.

Across the expanse there's a lonely cactus. I go to it, sit on the ground in its shade, pull out the list. They are all foreign-sounding names, but I don't recognize where they could come from. The paper folded back up, I lie on my back and close my eyes, hoping that sleep may wake me up.

The darkness my mind dives into makes way for light as I swim past the images and sounds of my subconscious, reaching the surface of the water gratefully, the distorted sun shining above it. But when my eyes open, I'm still in the desert.

"What?" I sit up and scan the surroundings. Perhaps this was where I actually lay down to sleep in the real world. But of course it's not. The sun is low in the reddish sky, its heat now weighing on me. My clothes stick to my body, sweat beading on my skin. Tumbleweed rolls by, as if attesting to my aloneness, flipping me the birdie. I flip it back.

Feeling like I've napped too long, I rub my eyes, slick my hair back, and spit my sleepy breath into the sand where it disappears with a sizzle. There's nothing to do but try to get out of this place, I suppose, so I make my way to where the ground slopes upwards, hoping I will better see where I am, and where to go, from here.

"You're dreaming, Edie. You know that," I tell myself out loud, dragging my feet in the sand. "So just decide: you'll see the town beyond this hill."

And when I get there, it's as I've chosen it: the town is there, spread before me, maybe a half-hour walk from the base of the hill. I can see my street on the outskirts, my new rich-lady house almost waving at me. Instead of conjuring up a motorbike, or another taxi, I decide to walk home.

Home: where I'm sheltered from the elements, where there is food and water, where I can play my records. Home is where my shit is. Any of those houses down there could be home. They are to someone else, where they find their bacon and eggs, their favourite jeans, their pet canary Maximilian. Having entered the circuit of streets, I stop and stare up at a window where the said canary is beating against the glass like a fly in a jar.

My daze is broken by a meow. And another. Walking down the street, my attention is drawn to kittens. Kittens, in every tree I cross, nested in the leaves, meowing to get the hell down. So I climb. Gripping branches and nubs, I pull myself up, scoop up the fur balls, and set them free at the bottom. From tree after tree, lining the quiet neighbourhood blocks, I rescue these helpless felines. There are so many, you wonder what the hell they were thinking. Accepting a dare from the neighbourhood dogs? But that couldn't be. Cats are their own kings. You can't bully them. They rule whatever space they occupy, unapologetically.

I help them down. I even rescue a cat that looks just like my street tabby, little "M" on its forehead, black-and-white fur splotched around his body. And I wonder if it's really him, lost in another neighbourhood. I don't feel like a hero or anything, getting them down. Actually, I couldn't care less. This is a dream. These cats aren't really in trouble. It's just something to do. So I do it.

By the time I arrive at my house, the sun is down. Behind me, a small galaxy of tiny bright orbs flash in the moonlight. Cat eyes. They followed me home. All of them.

"What do you want, cats? I got you out of your trees!"

I unlock my door with keys I pull out of my magical pockets. I turn to the cats again.

"Shoo! I don't have any milk, ok?"

That's a lie. I have milk, and I'm sure they know it. Cats are cunning creatures. I rub my face up and down a few times.

"Fine! Fine! Come in, you stinking, fluffy ninjas."

The place is the same in this dream as it is in my waking life. Full of stuff. So much stuff. It feels foreign and yet so goddamn satisfying. I try to turn on the living room light, but the switch doesn't work, so I pound it with my fist until the crystal chandelier comes to life, sending glittery diamonds onto the walls and floors.

The moon, bright and full, sets the grey skies aglow and bathes the yard in nacre light, clearly exposing every shape, and the doings of any skulking critter. That's why it's easy for me, though surprising, to see a man down there hardly trying to hide his intrusion. He sits by my empty pool, chucking things in, casually, like one would pebbles into a lake. I make my way down.

"Hello, Sir," I say. "What you got there?" I realize it's James. Salt-and-pepper-shaker James.

"Oh, hi Edie. Just throwing in these little rocks I found." He throws a few to demonstrate.

"Can I see?"

He opens his palms and shows me a handful of teeth. My stomach clenches with nerves. Taking his hand, I dump its contents into my own as if he was a child who has just been caught with poisonous berries.

"Look, James, you need to leave. This is private property. I'm keeping these rocks. They belong here."

"But I like them!"

He tries to grab them back, but I hold my hand up high where he can't reach. He gets up, and instead of going for my upheld fist, he lunges for me, his fingers curled like hooks. Digging them into my shoulders, he pushes me backwards.

"What the fuck, James!"

Without thinking, I slam my elbow into his face, his jaw cracking with the impact. The face that turns back around is dark with rage. His fingers, having released my shoulders with the blow, now aim for my neck. Swatting at his arms, I drop the teeth in the grass, stumbling further back until I'm almost against the house. He approaches, too rapidly, leaving me no time figure a way out.

If I die here, in coo-coo dreamland, that's the end, isn't it?

It's too late. He's got me now. Tightening around my throat, his hands are suddenly so hot they scorch my skin, the smell of barbecued pork climbing up my nose. I scream in pain, in panic. As if it was a call to my troops, the army of cats that had perched on my sofas and bookcases comes rushing forth through the screen door. Clawing up his legs and attacking every bit of his exposed skin with their sharp teeth, they cover him like a horde of hungry ants on a defenceless fledgling fallen from his nest, with no hope of flying away, slowly getting gnawed until it surrenders to death. Kittenish roars and meows finally subdue the man's pleas for help, and I step away, disgusted but thankful, from the blood-covered felines now feasting on the innards of his fallen body.

I make my way back upstairs, and, all at once so very sleepy, crawl onto one of the couches. Under a pink cashmere blanket I disappear.


Purring critters rub their bodies up and down my limbs. It seems the days when the sun acts as my alarm clock are over. This morning I have these cute killers luring me awake, summoning me to my feet. Tomorrow it might be Maximilian the canary, pecking at my face.

I pour the cats some fresh water in a long glass dish and place it in the middle of the floor. There are at least fifty of them, all piling over each other to get their share. Obviously they need to wash down the big James they feasted on last night.

I touch my neck. The burn, though tender, is healed over and feels like a tight scarf.

"Fucker."

Stepping onto the balcony, I crane my neck over the railing to see the remains I expect are sprawled below, but there is nothing. Have the cats eaten the bones too? More importantly, did they eat the real James? The James I knew would never have attacked me, not even if I had been holding a shiny napkin ring instead of teeth. But, then again, people can be surprising.

Finding no evidence after inspecting the yard, nor hidden away in the cedar hedges, I check the bags of teeth in the shed. One of them is open. I knot it shut.

The list of names is still in my pocket and I decide I shouldn't waste any more time. My new computer, still smelling of plastic and rubbing alcohol that electronics stores all smell like, hums to life. Into the search bar I type: Ruvila Zufo. All that pops up: Deceased, 1913. I try Havi Kojula. Deceased, 1913. Pareny Kojula (a relative to Havi?). Deceased, 1913. On went the list, each name as colourful as the last, all deceased in 1913. If that wasn't weird enough, they all came from a small island called Luumore. The island of the pink pills.

I type Luumore next, thinking perhaps the deceased's family members should be contacted. Maybe there are answers there. But Luumore doesn't come up anywhere, just as I remember it hadn't when I looked it up on my phone a million years ago. There was only minimal information in the pamphlet that came with the pills. Peering both with my eyes and with my mind around the room full of fancy junk, I give up before even lifting a finger. I wouldn't be able to locate it even were I to turn the place upside down.

It doesn't matter. There was nothing useful in the pamphlet. Only a description of the plant used to make the pill, the cursed pill that began all this mess and that somehow is now unnecessary for its continuation. I have been lucid dreaming all the same without it.

One, two three, four, five ... I have five fingers on each hand, my clocks all show 7 a.m., and I have half a hundred cats. My place is relatively clean, filled with everything I need, plus or minus some thousands of teeth. Way more than a dozen villagers' worth. But what can I do now? Fetch more from the bags and chase down another tooth scientist? I need a break. I need to scavenge through some vinyl records.

# FIFTEEN

A minute in the dreamworld feels like hours, days even, to the dreamer, and I've been spending all my nights actively exploring it, fully lucid. So it's only natural that it feels like decades since I've been to the Spin Factory, though it's only been a few days. The door is open, as it usually is when it's nice out. Like a long-lost adventurer coming back to her old stomping grounds, I walk in feeling both shy and excited. I scan the place for Wolf.

Near the far end, his back to me. I recognize his build. He's standing in front of a girl, who's red hair falls in curls over his arms, his arms that are wrapped around her waist. Of course. I shouldn't have expected anything less. I urged her on myself. Opened the door. Gave her the keys. Shot the arrow. Well, there you have it.

Suddenly, I feel quite stupid. As I turn to leave, Wolf catches sight of me.

"Edie!"

Though I want to ignore him, because I could—I have no need to ever see him again, and I know how to shut all the circuity of emotion to and from my heart with a snap—I stop, and turn. May is practically beaming, but Wolf looks embarrassed. I give him the most approving smile I can.

"Edie," he says again, giving me a big hug. I keep my arms at my side until he lets me go.

"Hi," I say.

"What's up with your neck?"

"Oh, this? I pulled my scarf off too fast. Major rug burn."

"And your arms?"

"Henna."

"Ok. Where have you been?"

"I moved, knucklehead. And quit my job."

"Yes, but I thought I'd still see you, that you'd come and buy records. It's been months."

"It hasn't been months."

"Uh, yes it has."

I look at May, who is right behind him now. She nods in agreement.

"What?" I pull out my phone and check my calendar. It's mid-September. It should be early July. Standing in the middle of the shop, in the middle of what feels like my old life, I have an awful feeling that I've forgotten something really important. As if I left the stove on, but worse. Much worse. I look up at Wolf with fear-stricken eyes. "Olive."

Running to the bus stop, biting my nails like a squirrel waiting for the next one, and then running all the way to the Cedar Residence, I show up drenched in sweat and out of breath.

"Edie," the nurse says. "We've missed you."

"Olive, can I see her?"

The nurse gives me a small smile, one that looks like a comforting tap on the back. I don't want to assume I know what's coming next. I don't want to know what her dumb-ass, back-tapping smile is for.

"I'm afraid you've missed her."

"I do miss her," I say, purposely not catching on. There's nothing to catch on to, anyway. "I miss her terribly." I'm only realizing it now.

"She's gone, Edie. She's taken flight."

"Oh, she has? Right. Ok. Thank you." I speak as nonchalantly as I can, as if she'd just told me Olive had gone out to buy some peanut butter and would be back in a short while. Maybe a long while. I swallow hard, forcing the ball of heat in my chest to stay put until I can make it back outside, but by the time my hand is on the handle, I can't see properly. The world is blurry, as seen through a rain-streaked window, fogged up with the contrast of inner heat and the icy coldness of the world.

The door closes on its own behind me. Around back is a small wooded area past the fenced-in yard. I find a nook and sit at the base of a tree.

And there the floodgates open. For an endless hour, sobs and heaves are the only sounds that travel through the thicket. Covering my mouth with my hand, I muffle wails for a stranger that became my family, my friend, the only human I ever really looked forward to seeing. She's not the first person I've lost, but she's the first I didn't want to lose.

I've been abandoned before. I've been humiliated. I've been beaten. This is different. This is a new pain. But it's all she left me, so I hold it tight, tight in my fists, keeping it close, letting it burrow, deep into the folds of my heart, where it will be safe, nestled with the other hardened stones of hurt hiding in there.

A calmer breath finds me, eventually, and I pick myself up from the ground. Even after the dirt from my hands is wiped on my pants, my hands are still stained. I count my fingers out of habit and shove them in my pockets. There's a tight roll of money in one and a handful of teeth in the other. How messed up am I? But it doesn't bother me. Olive passing leaves me caring about very little, and after the downpour of tears, there's not much left inside this shell that can be moved to feel.

Back home with all my shiny stuff and gazillion cats, I flop into a baby-blue, velour-covered, ornately carved Victorian armchair. It all suddenly seems more pointless than ever. My fancy home, my weird dreams, even the teeth and the dead cat-food man; it's all ethereal soup. A big swirl of mud and nothingness. Intangible chaos in a meaningless life.

"Let's drink," I tell a cat that has been purring its way into my dark existentialism. From the liquor cabinet, I pull out a whiskey bottle and pour some in a tumbler, carelessly spilling just as much onto the counter. The cat laps it up.

"Oh, you like that, huh? Well, then." I pour the rest of the bottle into their communal water dish. The carnivorous cats rush to it. I lift my legs, trying to not step on one as I leave them to it. I throw back my drink, pull out another bottle, refill the tumbler, and chug that one, and another, and another, until it doesn't burn my throat anymore, until my life feels tolerably ordinary, and I can bear to kick my feet up.

Elvira chooses a movie for me, some critically acclaimed happy bullshit. I change it to the 1958 horror flick Attack of the 50 Foot Woman. I watch and laugh, drinking straight from the bottle with my family of drunken cats.

The show ends and infomercials begin. I stumble to the light switch and my fingers run right through it. It won't click. A telltale sign that I'm in a dream. I count my ash-stained fingers. There are ten. I look at the digital clock. The time says 1 a.m., clear and bright. The analog one reads the same time, even after double checking. I try the light switch again. My fingers still swipe through without catching on any edge. The ultimate test, I push my index finger towards the palm of my other hand. It rests against solid flesh. Good, I think. But no, it keeps moving and pierces right through.

My drunken mind finds itself questioning the past days, wondering what in the hell was real, and what wasn't. There's no way of telling now. I grab my phone to dial up Wolf, but I forget his number. When my fingers succeed in pulling out my contacts, I see I've entered none.

"Well, then. I *won't* call you," I tell my phone. After staring at it for a few seconds, I decide to call up Jax Teller. He's my celebrity crush and I know *his* number by heart, because that's just how things are.

"Jax!" I drunkenly bellow. "I need you. Come over!" I toss my phone somewhere to my left and stumble up to my bedroom. When I get there, Jax Teller is already sprawled on my mattress.

"You're so ... quick!" I say with a hiccup. He pulls me to bed and I let him have his way with me.

My cats are the only ones with me in my sun-drenched room come morning. It's nice to have the golden heat wake me, and I wonder what day, what year, what world I'm in. My phone isn't anywhere to be found, so I do without. Showering brings an ounce of clarity, but no feeling. I'm an empty tumbler.

The house is tidy. I'm glad to see nothing crazy happened last night. Images flash through my mind as I think back, and I blush.

The cats are all hungover. You'd think if they could handle eating a full-grown man, they could handle their booze. Apparently not. Their food and water replenished, I head over to the liquor cabinet to take care of myself. The first bottle my hand grabs is good enough for me, though I bring it close to my face and go, "Mmm-hmmm," like I know what the hell I'm looking at. I pour the stuff and walk over to my front door in my housecoat, drink in hand. On the mirror in the entrance is a yellow sticky note. It reads: "I had a great time. J." I laugh out loud and step out onto the polished cement front stoop.

It's warm out, and the air is not too humid, not too fresh. Just right. I decide to walk around a bit, just down the block, just to enjoy it. A few stares come at me, what with me being barefoot, in my bathrobe, burnt neck, and a drink in my dark, stained hand. At least my hair is clean. I grab a strand to smell check. Clean.

I wave to a few onlookers, hoping to make them feel uncomfortable for staring. But then I catch a glimpse of my cats behind me. My fifty felines are all in tow, following me around the block. Well, the stares are justified, then. I wave all the same.

Instead of looping around, I keep going down another block, and another. My feet are sore and my drink has long been drunk, the tumbler tossed in a rosebush a few blocks back.

A flash of red and blue lights. The short, ascending sound of a rumbler siren cut short accompanies the gentle crunching of car tires slowly rolling up beside me.

"Ma'am," the policeman says to me, his window rolled down. My pace doesn't slow though I hear him. Instead I walk faster, thinking perhaps he's easing his way into an arrest for the unreported death by lightning of a whole village in my swimming pool. I consider making a run for it.

"Ma'am!" This time his voice booms through the PA system. I stop and turn.

"Ma'am, you need to go home," he says without the amplification. His hat is tucked low on his head and his sunglasses reflect my big, bathrobed shape. Only the lower part of his face is really his, and it looks sort of mean. He steps out and my heart skips a beat. He's going to cuff me. But instead he opens the door to the back seat.

"I'll feel like a criminal if I sit back there, Officer," I tell him with a twang of southern charm, an automatic response to him calling me "Ma'am".

"Don't worry, Ma'am, we just want to get you home safe, ok? Climb in."

My feet hurt and are black as dirt, so I get in without much coaxing. My furry friends hop in one after the other, and I am up to my neck in kittens.

"Make sure you keep those cats contained, now," the policeman says as he drops me in front of my house. "They're cute and all, but I'm not too sure it conforms with the law, having that many cats. I'll come 'round later this week to see what needs be done, Miss Porridge. Have a good day, now."

I'm bouncing with giggles all the way to my door, thinking that Edie Porridge is a mighty fine fake name to have given the policeman. Sometimes you have to get your laughs where you can. The cats rush in through the gap between my legs, multiplying my giggles. By the time I get to the main room, they've already surrounded a trespasser.

"Breaking and entry." I nod, impressed. "Stand down, kitties. He's a friend."

Wolf watches the cats disperse to all corners of the room, shaking his head in disbelief.

"Where the hell did you get all these cats?"

"How the hell did you get into my house?"

"The door was wide open."

"Oh." I walk over to the liquor cabinet and pull out another bottle and two tumblers. "Drink?"

"No thanks. It's nine in the morning."

I fill the tumbler and sit with my legs crossed, like a proper lady, in my great, big ol' Victorian armchair.

"So, whatchyou doin' pokin' your nose around in this here neighbourhood, sonny?"

Wolf frowns, caught off guard by my beguiling accent. "I just thought I'd visit, after yesterday being so weird."

"That was yesterday?"

"Yup."

"Hmm."

The sun is bright. Golden particles of dust float around me like pixie dust. I swoosh my hand through them. They move around but don't really go anywhere. Tightening my bathrobe, I get back up for a refill.

"So, are you with May?" I ask him, keeping my eyes on my glass. The question makes him uneasy, I can tell.

He walks around, looking over the various shiny trinkets that crowd every surface of every kind.

"Kind of."

I throw back another drink and slam it down harder than I mean to. Neither of us speaks for a few moments. I stare at the counter and finally turn to face him.

"Is this a dream?"

"I don't think so. Are you ok, Edie? Do you need help?"

"I don't think so."

"Why are you walking around town in your bathrobe?"

"The air was nice."

"Maybe you've had enough to drink for now."

"Maybe."

We both sit down.

"I gotta say, I'm surprised at how quickly you settled into your new life. It's all very ... fancy."

"You like it?"

"I'm not too sure. But obviously you're having fun, so ... power to you." He reaches into the messenger bag he had set down beside him and pulls out a plastic bag. "I brought you a few records."

There's that kindness again. This time I cradle it. I drink it up. I don't care. I stretch my hands out for my gift like a child. Red Hot Chili Peppers, Herbie Hancock, Debussy, and ...

"Phil Collins?" I burst out laughing.

"Your hundreds of copies were all burnt."

I put it on immediately and start doing a little dance, a little swinging of the hips and moving of the feet. I beckon him with my finger, and he doesn't hesitate to join.

When the needle hits the groove-less inner circle and the arm sets itself back on its armrest, we sit back down too, sweaty and smiling.

"Thanks, that was fun," I tell him.

"Can I ask you something?"

"Shoot."

"Who's J?"

"Who?"

"The sticky note on the mirror. Over there." He points towards the exit.

"Ah, that. I'm pretty sure that was a dream. I might have written the note myself, for all I know. Let's just say he was my May, for one night." I look at my dirty bare feet, sigh, and look back up. "Have you had May for one night, too?"

"Wow, Edie. Still as blunt. Well, not really. I went to her place, once. She was very insistent. We made out, a bit. But my head wasn't in it, and I had to leave. May is sweet and all, but she just seems like a distraction."

"From your ex-wife?"

Wolf closes his eyes.

"From you," he says, opening them now. "May is a distraction from you, and how much I miss you. It's been weird, not seeing you every day."

A small burst of butterflies flitters in my core. I haven't felt them in so long, it almost sobers me on the spot.

"Drink?" I say.

"No. Listen." He slides off the couch and comes over to me on his knees. His eyes are level with mine, his hands on top of my hands resting in my lap. "I want *you.*"

I think about this for a moment. Because I might be drunk, and I might be tangled up with some weird, reality-skewing dreams, but one thing I am not is romantic. I have no need for it, and I don't trust it. Foolish and misleading emotions get the best of us and drag us down roads so quickly that by the time we realize we've taken a wrong turn, we're lost. We're lost so deep, with no reception to call for help, stuck with the true face that hid so well behind the flowers, the kindness, the sorcery. Romance is irrational. Now passion, on the other hand, is logical. You can feel it, feed it, and be done with it. It's raw, and it's honest.

And love, well, that's a rare thing I think no one really comes across in their life unless they've sold some part of themselves to the devil. Which is why they cling onto the other person, since they are no longer complete, and need to fill the void to feel whole.

"Edie?"

"Sorry. So, *you want me*, like, you wanna make out? Because we can do that. If you want."

"I want you, as a lover, as a partner, as a friend."

"Ya. Shit. That's different."

I slip out from under his hands and out of the armchair and walk towards the fridge.

"I think you should go." I open it, looking for some kind of food I could throw at him if need be.

"Not this again," he says, standing. "What happened to you, Edie? Why are you so afraid?"

"I ain't afraid of shit." I turn around, suddenly angry. I want to throw insults at him, tell him stuff I shouldn't, stuff that would hurt him, to stop the gushy garbage coming out of his mouth. If he says "I love you" I think I'll throw the eggplant I'm holding.

"I love you," he says.

I throw the eggplant at his head. He bats it away with both arms.

"Get out!" I yell.

"Ok! But it changes nothing. You're my favourite person, and you can't do anything about it. You can't hide behind all your peacocky shit," he says, pointing around. "You've got a million cats and you take walks around town in your bathrobe. You're a total weirdo! Of course your love life isn't going to be normal. How could it? And that's a fantastic thing!"

"You know nothing of my love life!"

"I know that you didn't write that note on the mirror! That's not your handwriting at all! And you know what? That's ok, because it's none of my business." He picks up his messenger bag. "I'll be outside while you cool off."

"What?"

Wolf leaves. Not sure I fully understand what he means by "I'll be outside" (perhaps it's code for getting the hell out of my life), I look through the front door's peephole. I can't see him. I open the door a tiny crack and peek. He's sitting on my stoop, his back to me, facing the street. Quietly clicking the door shut, I tiptoe back to the kitchen.

Over the next few hours, I periodically look through the bathroom window, from which I can see the stoop, to see if he's gone. His ass seems to be glued to the steps. For some reason, his presence bothers the crap out of me, so I try to drown him out by blasting the most aggressive music I can find, hoping the frequencies bump him off, and away. I scream and yell along to the music, banging on surfaces with wooden spoons. His butt-glue seems soundproof, and it's driving me nuts.

Finally I turn the noise-music off and decide to write him a note. A polite note, asking him to simply leave my stoop. Courtesy can be so effective in tense situations. Wrapped over itself into a grade-school fold-and-tuck pattern, a note reading "Get the fuck off my stoop" is flung through the door crack. I rush to the bathroom window to watch him unfold it. He reads, looks up to the window from which I'm spying, and gives a thumbs up.

"Yes," I cheer.

He picks up his bag, goes down the steps, along the little cobblestone path, and out into the street. He's gone. I feel a tug of sadness, as if we were playing a game I expected to lose, but I grunt it clear out of my system and stomp back into the kitchen.

Even though I'm in no way hungry, I make myself a lethargic lunch. It doesn't taste like much.

# SIXTEEN

Kitty litter is gross, but I clean it because my cats poop real poop. In fact, dream or not, it all blends into each other. So I need to take both worlds equally seriously. They have become one and the same. I cannot have fake, dreamworld kittens and real kitty poop. It doesn't add up.

There are still a few hours left in the day, and not much I can do about teeth or Wolfless stoops, so I decide to throw a party, because I don't feel like being alone with my thoughts in an empty room. I'd rather be alone in a crowded room; it's easier to not think. Watching other bodies can be so satisfyingly distracting, no matter what they're doing. And my cats don't count. They don't do much other than sleep, and watch *me*. I guess I'm *their* distraction.

Finding my phone under the couch, I look through the contact list. It's empty, because I haven't transferred the numbers over from my old phone. Also, because I don't have any friends. There were only four numbers on my old phone: Wolf, Emily, Todd, and the Cedar Residence, and even if I knew them by heart, they'd be useless.

"All right then." I throw the phone back to the floor. "Plan B."

Making a bee-line for my bedroom, I pull out a clothes hanger from the closet. A black dress. I throw it on the bed and pull out another. A long, black blouse. I chuck it aside. The same goes for garment number three and all the others until my closet is empty. I don't remember buying any of these clothes. I don't usually wear dresses.

A mountain of black fabric domes my bed.

"I have nothing to wear."

Having to choose *something*, I close my eyes and shove my black arms into the pile, deciding to pick whatever gets extracted. It's a black dress. But it has pockets, so luck is on my side. I strip and slip into it, and run downstairs.

"Cats, be good!" I yell as I grab my purse and jump into some sneakers. "I'm going out!"

I walk down to the first busy road that crosses mine and hail a cab.

"Where to?"

"The fanciest club you know!" If I can, then why not? I think to myself.

"The Studded Lemur?"

"Whatever you say!"

We stop in front of a brick building painted black, bright amber light bulbs lining the top of the wall. A hefty tip to the cab driver, some human eye contact, and I step out.

A black-domed awning arches over an open door, white fairy lights hung along the edge and down the poles supporting it, shining like diamonds against the dark backdrop. Sharply clad individuals are lined up, waiting to be ushered through a gloomy entrance; a black hole from which they might never re-emerge the same. I stare, impressed by the seriousness of it all.

A few strangers glare, scrutinizing me. I'm suddenly glad my sneakers match my dress (because I could have chosen the bright red ones without caring less). Unfortunately, so do my arms. They are still as black as can be, and having people stare at them only revives the bleak memory of the zapped villagers, the floating ash, the bobbing teeth, and the eaten James. But I'm out here to forget that, so I brush off the demeaning looks. Let them think I'm just a rich kook.

"I'm a rich kook," I tell a tall blond standing in line in front of me. She's wearing black, as I am. As most are. It certainly looks chic, but it also gives the impression that the rich are forever mourning something. I'm just glad my wardrobe fits the part.

When my turn finally comes, I hand the doorman a hundred dollar bill. He lets me through without a second look.

Past one black, velvet curtain is a dazzlingly lit room, long and narrow and lavishly decorated, its brilliance contrasting with the black exterior of both the building and the night itself. A bar runs along the left wall and mirrors panel the right one. The white ceiling is domed and at least fifteen feet high, decorated with gilded leaves and swirls. Everything sparkles or reflects sparkles, making every nook seem encrusted with gems.

The chairs and barstools are all upholstered with white leather, their legs painted gold.

Amongst the shimmering glitter are the black-clad people, standing with perfect postures. Every so often, someone throws their head back in boisterous laughter, a sound so fake it reeks. It's the proof they must impress on others that they belong. A laugh. To show that they are comfortable, that they are fun, and that they think you're funny, too. You, in turn, will appreciate them for appreciating you. I think of this and try a small, fake laugh to myself. I sound like an idiot.

A few heads turn to look, only to lift their noses at me and dip them back into their drinks, whipping their hair like it could sweep the trash that I am away from them.

I walk up to the bar.

"Give me something strong, please." I lean over the counter to better project my voice to the bartender. He is dressed in a tuxedo, clean shaven, his hair cut neat, and looking like he showered just minutes before his shift. He turns to me and smiles.

"Sunset Rum?"

"Sounds divine."

He hands me a fancy cocktail glass with limes tucked in on the side. My drink is orange and looks like it should be drunk by a pool at an all-inclusive beach resort.

"Great," I say, unsmiling.

"I'm sorry, would you like something different?"

"No, it's fine. I just wanted something to kick my teeth in. This looks like it'll tickle my tongue and make me giddy."

"That doesn't sound so unpleasant," he says. "You're much too pretty to lose teeth over a drink."

I give him the usual distrusting leer I give any stranger being too friendly for no reason, and remember that it's his job to be nice, just like mine was once upon a time.

"Ya, sure. Hey, what's back there?" I point to the far back, where I see more curtains.

"That's the lounge. There's a dance floor, some booths. A bar."

I thank him and step down.

"Watch out for those pretty teeth," he says.

There's a creepy twinkle in his eye, giving me an odd sense of the dreamworld. I count my ash-stained fingers. One, two, three, four, five. They are bit blurry but I have the right number. It could just be the alcohol. My drink in hand, I walk through the gem-studded room, my chin jutted out to deflect the stares, all the way to the large black curtains in the back which I hurriedly push aside. I do hate the snootiness.

The light is much dimmer here and my eyes take a few seconds to adjust. I feel like I have stepped into a parallel universe. The way my life is going, I wouldn't be surprised to learn this was a portal into the *Mos Eisley Cantina*.

Instead of white and mirrored, here the walls and floors are black, and the ceiling low. The lights are a dull orange, spaced few and far between.

Waiters move languidly from table to bar, and bar to table. Decked in black from head to toe, their hairdos vary from fuchsia cornrows, to vibrant green spikes, to mustard yellow mop-tops. All of them have their faces covered in a sort of white talc, and their eyes are darkened from their eyebrows down to their cheekbones, like pandas. One of them shows me the way in with a graceful wave of the hand.

Semi-private booths gather clusters of barflies around small glass tables. I walk past them, taking notice of the champagne glasses from which everyone seems to be drinking, each brimming with silvery liquid. On the tables are crystal bowls filled with white, glittering jewels. Hands reach in and scoop up handfuls, popping the little chunks into their mouths like peanuts or jelly beans. The people seem relaxed, and perhaps slightly morose. One dark-haired man, unusually tall, noticeable even sitting because of how much higher his head and shoulders reach past the others beside him, invites me over with a strangely classy flop of the wrist. I oblige.

"Come, sit. Eat. Be merry," he says with melancholy, flicking a gem into his mouth with the tips of his long, bony fingers. The crunch it makes sounds like dry, hard chalk between his teeth, giving me unpleasant shivers.

I squeeze in at the edge of the black, leathery bench beside a red-haired lady of voluptuous beauty, the top of her breasts bulging out of her dress but buried under necklace upon necklace of pearls. The diamonds and blood-red rubies garnishing her fingers from first to last knuckle compete for attention as she taps her fingertips on the glass tabletop.

A stack of hundred dollar bills is placed at the centre of the table, a skin peeled from it every so often by some fingers just as bedazzling as the ones belonging to the lady beside me. The bill is then rolled like a cigarette with some jelly bean gems at its centre, and eaten like a burrito.

"Does that taste good?" I ask the tall man chewing on the money burrito. His mouth full, the person next to him answers instead.

"Completely decadent." Both smile, their eyes glassy, their teeth and lips slick with silver.

None is offered to me, so I imagine I am supposed to help myself. I hesitate. Looking around for some sort of permission, I find it in my red-haired neighbour, who nods at me with happy, squinting eyes. She closes them then, and swings her head back, thrusting her chest out with a soft grunt. I'm thinking there must be something really potent in these candy gems. But I see something moving under the glass table and realize it's not the gems that are making her squirm. Someone is under there, pleasuring her. I sprint up from my seat, but not without a handful of edibles.

I keep threading among the booths. Things are happening in this dark room, above and below the tables, without sound but with obvious delight. Everyone is getting off on something.

The dance floor is empty.

*rachel tremblay*

"Why is there no music?" I ask a waiter passing by.

"No need, baby bird. No need."

"If there were, there'd be people dancing."

"Birdie baby, the music is in here." He puts his fingertip to his temple.

"Whatever. Give me a drink, please?"

He gives me one of the silver-filled flutes from his tray. I reach into my pocket to pay.

"No need, baby bird. It's on the house."

I nod a thanks and gulp it all down. It's thick and warm, and tastes of honey with a strong, metallic aftertaste.

It makes me gag, and I'm instantly intoxicated.

There is a pleasant softness to my body. All at once, life feels like a delicate rose petal; easily enjoyed but easily destroyed. My senses are heightened. The smoky, sweaty, and fragrant smells, the feel of the satin dress on my skin, the bumpy-looking texture of the walls. All are sharply defined in my mind and feel as close and familiar to me as my own breath. My deep joy and my even deeper sadness are palpable, gently squirming in me like a child in the womb.

At once, I fit in. The darkness and its strange crowd feels more like home than the stuffy, bright room on the other side ever would.

My legs move easily, right onto the black-and-red checkered dance floor. My arms float up, my body twirls, and I dance alone, soundless, feeling so delicious I could almost *get off* without anyone crawling under my glass table. I think I just might.

I pull at my hair, the world spinning as I turn and turn, until, losing all its features and its occupants at the same time, the room starts closing in on me.

Stunning me out of my ecstasy, I watch the black walls move inwards, noiselessly. They come closer and closer, stopping only a few feet away. Instead of being hard, as walls should be, they are now curved, and soft like cloth, making it seem like I'm standing in a big black bag. A knee-high chunk of ruby sits beside me. It's meant to keep me warm. I understand this, though I know it never could.

"Hey!" A waiter's head pops over the top edge of the cloth wall, a hundred feet up. "You want to get out? You need to attract a bird!"

"What? Why?"

"Because! You're trapped!"

I shrink down and sit on the ground, wondering if my dreams will ever make any sense. Because this is a dream, obviously, and it doesn't make sense. Dreams can be so cryptic. Perhaps I'm supposed to understand something about this place. These people. I know for sure this stupid ruby won't keep me warm. And I know I can't really eat money, silver, or jewels. Even though they just might get me off.

My pockets are full of gems, and I consider passing the time by munching on a few. Before I can do this, a squawk and a muffled flapping tumbles from above. A white bird, a chicken, lands with a thud, just inches from the ruby.

"You crazy shit!" I yell upwards. "You could have killed it!"

"What do you care?" I hear in a faint echo.

"Why wouldn't I?" I yell back.

Poor animal. I pick it up in my arms and bring it close to my chest. It turns its head to me and I shriek. It has Wolf's face.

I startle awake on my couch. It's not surprising to discover it was all a dream. What I wonder is: When did I fall asleep? When was my last false wake up? I reach into my little black dress's pockets and pull out a handful of gems from each, dropping most of them onto the floor. The cats come rushing.

"Great."

Shuffling over to the broom closet at the entrance, I see a yellow sticky note still clinging to the mirror. Filled with sudden disgust, I go to pull it off. But it's not Jax's scribbles on it anymore.

*Call me. Whenever. Wolf.*

# SEVENTEEN

"Ya, well, I don't have your phone number." I yank the note down. Behind it are black sharpied numbers.

"Ruin a perfectly good mirror, why don't you."

I grab the broom and pick up what the cats haven't eaten of the gems and dump them in a nacre bowl on the coffee table, a few missing the target. Sitting on the couch, I pluck the rogue rocks from the table and drop them in, one by one, my thoughts elsewhere.

Controlling some to a certain extent, and completely losing my footing in others, drifting along in and out of these worlds is disorientating. The concept of time means nothing. I have no anchor. There's no north star to guide me. I'm lost. My compass is kaput, and everything seems to be stripped of meaning. Riches don't matter anymore. The dead villagers don't matter. My stupid cats don't matter. Sexual tomfooleries don't matter. There is no love in my life. No desire. Not to bone, not to eat, not to move, not to feel. I'm dried up. I don't care, about anything at all.

My body weighs a thousand tons and I cannot pull myself up from the couch. My mind blank, I sit there for what feels like an eternity, but which in reality is the time it took for the sun to travel from one end of the window-wall to the other. A ray smacks me in the eye and I resurface, feeling just as hopeless.

"Fuck it."

Flopping to my side and using gravity to roll off the couch, I crawl on my hands and knees, searching for my phone amidst the paw-licking kitties. Most of them are lounging, as they always do—there's no telling if they got buzzed off those gems.

My phone is in the litter box.

I wipe it on my shirt and continue on all fours to the entrance. Stretching my neck as far as it can go without getting up, I can manage to see the numbers on the mirror. I dab the first few on my phone's keypad. I stretch to look again, I beep a few more numbers.

Stretch, poke. When it starts ringing I lie flat on my back.

"Hello," Wolf answers.

"It's me."

"Edie."

"Uh-huh."

"How are ya?"

"Off my feet."

"Is that a good thing?"

"I don't know. I can't tell. I can't tell anymore."

"You want me to come over?"

A pause.

Of course I'd like to think I don't care about this either. I'd like him to think I don't care. That I am a stalwart loner, and I need no one. But there's a glimmer, a faint one, far away. A tiny beacon. It signals to me. Letting me know, so that it might save me. There is need in this baby bird.

"I think so."

"I'll be there in twenty."

When he shows up, I am lying on my back, a starfish, in the middle of the living area, kittens snuggled along my whole periphery and sprawled over random parts of my body. Kittens over my knees, in my armpits, across my neck. They have purred me to oblivion. I stare at the ceiling without seeing.

"Edie."

Hearing Wolf's voice triggers a small skip in my heartbeat and reminds me that I am not dead.

"That looks so comfy," he says, no concern in his voice. He's not worried about me. He doesn't know.

I blink and clear my dry throat. "I don't care about anything."

"Oh."

"I never know whether I'm awake or asleep anymore."

"Oh, shit."

"You think I'm going crazy?"

"I don't know. When's the last time you ate something?"

"What does that have to do with anything?"

"Well, do we ever eat in our dreams? Let me take care of you a bit."

I don't like those words at all, but I don't protest. Wolf makes a sandwich and places the plate beside my head on the floor. The cats all come to life then, so he picks it up and takes it to the coffee table by the couch instead.

"Come and eat this."

Seeing as I don't move, he comes and helps me, pulling me by the arms to a sitting position.

"Edie, what's going on."

"I told you."

"Ok, come." He slings my arm over his shoulder, lifts me to my feet, and guides me to the couch where he sets me back down. He leaves, and a few moments later I hear the comforting noise of a vinyl record coming through the speakers. Billie Holiday sings to me and a spark is struck in the dark recesses of my soul.

"I forgot about music," I say, drinking in the sounds, parched.

"How could anyone, especially you, forget about music? What does that even mean?"

I lean back and close my eyes. I feel my heart roar to life like a well-oiled engine.

"Wolf?" I keep my eyes shut, my head back.

"Yes?"

"My cats ate a guy."

"What?"

"He was trying to kill me. He had found the teeth."

"You were *attacked?*"

"The teeth are in the shed. You can go see."

"Did he hurt you?"

"Go see," I say again.

Wolf gets up and leaves. After a few moments of absorbing the music, I open my eyes and eat my sandwich. Wolf comes back, dragging one of the bags.

"What the hell is this?" he asks, more curious than alarmed. "There are *thousands* of teeth in here! And more out there!"

"They're villagers, from the island that made my sleeping pills. I watched them get zapped by lightning in the pool. It was horrifying." I say this, with no emotion, to my sandwich, though I remember quite well how horrifying it actually was. "That's all that's left of them. But there weren't that many in the water. The math doesn't add up."

I put my sandwich down and look halfway over my shoulder towards him.

"I ran the check on a handful of teeth, and they match. The strange thing is ..."

I turn back to my sandwich and pick it back up.

"The strange thing is, apparently they've all been dead for almost a century. And I can't find the island anywhere. There's no record of it."

I finish eating. Wolf drags the bag of teeth towards the couch and sits beside me.

"How did you get them traced? Does anyone know you found some hundred-year-old teeth in your backyard?"

"I didn't know they were that old. I got it done in a dream."

Wolf pinches the bridge of his nose.

"Edie, I don't know how to tell you this."

"No, I don't know how to tell *you*. We could have sex in a dream, and I could get pregnant in real life. That's how messed up things are right now."

"That's impossible, Edie."

"I know it sounds crazy. What's going on *is* crazy. But *I'm* not! I'm completely lucid."

Saying it with such conviction confirms it for me. I'm sane.

"Reality isn't what we think it is, Wolf. The mind, the mind …" I grab a handful of the gems from the nacre bowl. "I'm not going to pretend I know how it works. But my mind, since those damn pink pills, has obliterated the limits between what's material and what's … intangible. The tricky part is that it doesn't affect only me."

Wolf seems amused. A bit worried, but amused.

"So these teeth," he says, "they could belong to other people than those villagers, couldn't they? I mean, how trustworthy is data collected from your dreams?"

"As trustworthy as if I tell you that the plant I surprised you with a hundred years ago was from a dream, my five million dollars of insurance money was from a dream. This house! I found it and persuaded the owner to sell, in a dream! These diamonds, they're from a ritzy club I dreamed up, called the Studded Lemur. Not only are these things edible, but they will get you high."

Wolf chuckles and plucks one from my open hand. He tries to crush it with his nail. He shrugs.

"So you found some drugs."

"*From my dream*, Wolf. They were rolling these up in hundred dollar bills and eating them. And they were drinking silver." I remember my moment on the dance floor and my face flushes with heat. "That's where I was just now, before waking on my couch, with my pockets full of those."

"That's where you were." Wolf chuckles again.

"You think I'm nuts."

"No."

"Then what are you thinking?"

"That this couch is CRAZY comfortable."

"I know!" I say, trading the drama for a moment of levity. It doesn't last.

"What is it with rich people, Wolf?"

"What do you mean?"

"I mean, I'm rich now. But I don't feel like I am. The rich people in my dream, they were either snobs, or completely off their rocker, overcome with extravagance and a sort of devotion to pleasure. I kind of felt I fit better with the latter, but that's a recipe for disaster."

"Is that what you think of rich people? Only two options?"

"I don't know. That's all I really know about them."

Wolf held up the little gem to the light. "You asked me once if I was poor."

"Ya."

"You said that you were, or were before you got your money."

"Ya."

"Are you still poor, Edie?"

His question makes sense. I have all this *peacocky* shit, yet I still feel poor. I am deficient. Of something. Oh, they say real wealth is love, health, and friends. And maybe that's true, and that's why I'm poor. Because I don't really have those things. What I do have is music, I realize then, listening to Billie. And I am healthy, I think. At least until insanity pulls me down into perdition, if these dreams don't let up. And, in a way, I have Wolf.

"Thanks for coming over," I tell him.

Wolf pops the gem in his mouth and crunches down on it.

"What are you doing?" I panic.

"Testing your theory," he says, getting chunks out of his teeth with his tongue.

"Shit! Ok." I choose a diamond out of my handful and put it in my mouth, and let the other gems roll off the side of my palm back into the bowl. Almost breaking a few teeth in the process, I crunch mine. It tastes like aspirin and honey.

Clearing his throat, Wolf leans back, stretching his arms out along the top of the couch. He fiddles with my hair.

"Cut the crap," I tell him, about to lecture him about something, but I forget what. My body and thoughts become numb in one fell swoop. A blink, and the lack of feeling is replaced with a comfortable pleasure. Beside me, Wolf is smiling, all teeth exposed, looking mighty pleased.

# EIGHTEEN

"That was *fast!*"

Wolf bounces up to change the record, slipping another one out of his bag. Holding it at its edges, he lays it down with his fingertips, a loving flame in his eyes. The needle lands like a feather on water, and a crackle akin to that of a warm fire heats up the room.

"Those few dreams I've had with you, they were really something." He flops back onto the couch, closer to me this time. He lifts his feet to put them on the table, changes his mind, and leaves them on the rug. He sinks into the cushions a bit more and stares at the ceiling. "I guess they're more than just lucid dreams, huh?"

"You high?"

"I think so. I feel fuzzy and warm. And hungry. But not for food." He sighs.

"I know what you mean. I shouldn't have followed you down the rabbit hole." I sink lower into the couch too. "You know what I'd do, if I was really, really rich?"

"You *are* really, really rich."

"Yes, well, I mean *really* rich."

"What … would … you … do?" He moves his lips slowly, feeling the shapes his mouth makes.

"I'd buy all the armaments in the world. And then destroy them. Let people fight with their bare hands if they really must."

"Uh-huh. Smart. I'd … buy a spacecraft. And explore another galaxy."

"You know we'd all be dead by the time you came back, if you ever did come back."

"Ok, scratch that. How's this: I'd pay all the best scientists in the world to work for me, researching diseases and finding cures."

"Such philanthropy! Why would they need to work for you and not, I don't know, the government? Who do scientists work for anyway?"

"Not sure, but I'd have them work for me because *I'm* not corrupt. I'd make sure nothing good gets swept under the rug at the expense of making a buck. You know the pharmaceutical companies make their money off sick people, not off healthy ones."

"That's right. I've had my eye on them for a while."

"Your eye?"

"Yes, this eye." I point to my right eye. Wolf doesn't lift his head to see what eye I'm pointing at. "So, do you think those scientists of yours have other scientist friends? Because they could also work for *me*."

"Doing what?"

"Un-polluting the water."

"Un-polluting."

"Ya."

Wolf nods. "Ok, but don't you think we'd just pollute it again? And all that work would've been for nothing?'

"Well, it would be a fresh start, at least," I tell him.

"But that's just like making your bed every morning even though you know you're going to mess it up again."

"Exactly. And we do it anyway."

"Maybe you do." He laughs. "I need to start making my bed."

There's a pause while we stare at the ceiling in contemplation.

"We could make sure everyone has access to education, everywhere," he adds. "And not just reading and writing and shit. You can be brilliant, and still be a total asshole. I'm talking *soul* education."

"Spiritual education."

"Teach humanity right out of their racism, bigotry, and cruelty."

"And greed."

"Greed's a bitch."

Only now do I realize that we are holding hands.

"Wolf?"

"Ya?"

"Let's burn this fucker down."

Wolf turns his upper body towards me, his face an inch from mine.

"What do you mean, *this fucker*."

"My house. Screw this peacocky shit." I stare at him, unflinching at his nearness.

"But it's your house. You went through so much weird shit to get it."

"It means nothing."

Our eyes are locked, the humanity of it almost unbearable.

"You're high. You don't think you'll regret it?" He licks his lips.

"Maybe. Maybe not." I squeeze his hand.

His other hand dives into his pocket and pulls out a pack of matches. He holds them up without looking at them.

"You still hungry?" I ask him.

He flicks the matches on the table without looking and slips his hand behind my ear. I still don't flinch. But I'm a bit scared. And that's ok.

There is no knocking bowls off the coffee table, no tearing away clothes. A smile, the best green light of all, is all he needs as permission to kiss me. His eyes penetrating mine, I feel like I'm being spiritually undressed. But I don't look away. We strip down, and pull each other in, as naturally as cool rain seeps into the warm earth.

Meanwhile, the matches Wolf flicked ignite, all on their own, into a small puff of fire. We, the natural elements at play with the ebb and flow of flesh, are too absorbed to notice. The fire spreads to the little drug diamonds. They burst, one after the other, like miniature firecrackers. In minutes, the whole coffee table is aglow with flames. We finally pause to look.

"Hey," I say.

"Ya?"

"It's a tad early in the game, don't you think? It could have waited another hour, at least."

"It's beautiful though."

"It sure is."

We turn back to each other, focussing on the more important task at hand.

Meanwhile, the flames grow, consuming the wood until it starts falling in clumps onto the rug.

"The cats," I remember.

I arch my back over the couch's arm and watch, upside down, kitten after furry kitten run towards the kitchen. I swear they each shoot me a look as they pass, their eyes screaming: "Save yourself, woman!" I watch them go as best I can, and when they make it out onto the balcony, I let them be. I've got my own kind of saving to do.

The drapes rumble into brightness, passing the torch to each other left and right. The heat licks our skin and we slide back into rhythm, a wilder instinct taking over.

With sudden urgency, we tussle like wrestling animals, grappling with the shifting of sinew and

OFF MY FEET

softness, growls escaping our constricted throats. The smoke gets denser. Our grip gets tighter. It's getting harder to breathe. The fire rages angrier. The ceiling floods with a bright red whoosh, and the devouring blaze cradles us tighter, and tighter. Our skin sizzles.

Wolf howls through the thunder of the flames, his claws ripping through my hide as he pulls me forward. I thrust my fangs into his exposed neck. Blood, thick and warm, gushes into my roaring jaw. Spinning in a delirious vortex of crimson, our heat rises until we become ethereal, stretched between heaven and earth, dreaming and waking, untouchable, immortal, consumed.

The coat of blood on our skin protects us as we crawl out of the house through the small gap below the rolling wall of smoke and flames. We tumble off the stoop onto the cool grass and pull each other away from the house, gasping for clean air. I crawl into his arms, nesting my dizzy head in his bloody neck, and close my eyes, the red of the burning house shining brightly through my eyelids.

A blanket thrown over my shoulders, I'm being pulled to my feet by the time I realize Wolf has been pried away from me. I hadn't even heard the sirens.

# NINETEEN

"Let's get you to safety!" yells a firefighter. The cascade of noise coming from the conflagration hits my ears all at once, like the world's mute button has just been released. Pain signals reach my brain; my skin is blistering. Wolf is beside me. He meets my startled eyes with a smile and a wink, but I can tell he is sad.

Cleaned, robed, and minor burns cared for, we lie restless in neighbouring hospital beds, waiting for who knows what. Too dazed to speak, we watch the clock tick on the opposite wall for a million hours, until we are finally visited by a nurse and two policemen.

"We need to take your statements," says one cop. The other holds a clipboard and a form.

"We knocked over a candle having sex," Wolf answers before I had time to say anything. "It was *hot*."

I snap my head around to look at him.

"Sorry, I know it's a bad joke. It was impossible to resist," he says, his voice lowered.

The policeman scribbles away on his paper, unimpressed. He looks at me next. "Miss?"

"Yup. I mean, yes, that's correct. We were reckless. It's quite horrible isn't it? Are we in trouble, Officer?"

"Trouble? Well, you're lucky to have gotten out alive. And your house is gone. Otherwise, both of you need to come in to the station for questioning as soon as you're permitted to leave the hospital. The doctors've told us you'll be discharged tomorrow morning."

"Questioning about what, Sir?" I ask, nervously squeezing my blanket.

"Mostly about some remains that were found in the grounds." He clips his pen in place and looks up at both of us.

My heart sinks. I give him my most shocked face, which is easy because I am terrified.

"What?"

"Yes, Miss. It seems, according to what our team of forensic anthropologists have come up with, that your house was built on top of a mass grave."

"What the fuck?" Wolf and I say at the same time, the terror morphed into simple unbelief.

"Like I said, tomorrow."

The officers tip their hats and leave, receiving a nod and a smitten smile from the nurse who follows them out. Once alone, I flip onto my side with a small groan of pain.

"Wolf," I say. "Did you hear that? That's freaking amazing."

"How is that amazing?"

"Because I can't possibly be blamed for that. I'm off the hook! As long as they don't find James's bones."

Wolf gives me a questioning look.

"The man my cats ate," I say.

"You knew him?"

"He was an old neighbour. I still haven't looked up to see if he's gone for real."

"You don't seem too sad about it."

"He tried to kill me." I shrug.

"Maybe your cats ate his bones, too. Seems like they are crazy enough for that."

"Hey, don't diss the cats. They saved my ass."

"Ok, then."

"I wonder if they got out all right. I should have asked the cops."

I wriggle onto my back, the uncomfortable bed squeaking under me, and stare at the ceiling until I doze off.

When I wake, Wolf is already up, dressed, and eating an omelet. His table: a baby incubator.

"Good morning," he says with his mouth full. He points to a plate of eggs on my bedside table. I pick up the fork and move the food around on the plate without appetite. Tiny diamond nuggets surface from within the golden scramble.

"Did you put these in there?"

"Put what?"

"The gems?"

"No."

Suspicious, I look at the clock. There are four hands, all pointing in different cardinal directions.

"I'm dreaming," I mumble to myself, setting the fork down.

"What's that?"

"I'm fucking dreaming!" I yell.

"Good grief, relax."

Looking around, the room seems smaller than it was. And warmer. Maybe too warm.

"Ugh. It's cooking in here." I fan myself with my hand. There's something on the tip of my index finger. A white pimple.

"Wolf, come check this out."

I show him my finger. Without warning, he squeezes the white nodule. Instead of bursting, a long, white worm starts coming out. Wolf pulls on it. I can feel it, all through my finger, my hand, my arm, slowly sliding out. It's long and thin, and keeps getting longer as Wolf keeps pulling, stepping farther away as the worm is lured out from deeper and deeper within me. It tingles horrendously along the whole artery it moves through, sending shivers through my whole body, making my toes curl. Finally I feel it tugging at my heart. There's no more give. It's stuck, clawed in place. But Wolf keeps yanking. He tugs and tugs, and it hurts, but he won't stop, though I cry each time it jerks, from deeper within than anything could ever possibly be.

I scream. "STOOOOOP!"

I wake up in the hospital bed, sitting up straight, sweating.

"Fuck," I say, catching my breath.

The room is dark. Wolf's fast deep breathing blends with mine.

"Wolf?" I whisper.

"Are you ok?" he asks.

"You're awake?"

"Hell ya. That was crazy."

"You saw it?"

"I was there, Edie. I'm sorry. I couldn't stop pulling."

"I don't want to go back to sleep. Can I climb in with you?"

"Come here."

Scooching over a notch, he makes room for me to climb in. I snuggle up in the crook of his arm and keep my eyes open until morning.

Come dawn, I have no more patience for mass graves and white worms that tick-tick-tick with the clock. I wake Wolf up.

We get dressed in some donated clothes, our burns much milder than I would have expected, considering how long we were buck naked in that nest of flames.

You can really tell how much something hurts when you finally have to squeeze into clothing.

I taste my mouth and wish I had a toothbrush. Right on cue, the nurse shows up with disposable toothbrushes and reminds us that we need to go straight to the police station.

We sling on oversized jackets and shoes and shuffle down to the station.

There isn't much to be done. I sign the papers they tell me to sign. One of them confirms I bought the house from a Bob Blanchett, who bought it off a Stevie Grant, who is now deceased. Another has to do with my property now being a crime scene. I am to find another place to live, for an indefinite amount of time, and, though I own that slice of land, I have no claim to what they find in the ground.

We are lead into a small room.

"I'm Detective Sergeant Grunt. Please sit. We just want to bring you up to par," says a man in plain clothes, pulling out a chair for himself from under the steel interrogation table.

"About the mass grave, Sir?" I say.

"Yes." He strokes his beard a few times, examining us. "The remains are about a hundred years old. We're finding a lot of teeth, more teeth than a normal human being should possess, but still, they're human teeth. I need to ask: did you know anything about this?"

We both shake our heads.

"They've been traced to a small island called Luumore."

"Ha!" I exclaim.

The cop pulls his head back. "You know of this place?"

"Oh, well, I've heard of it."

He studies me with his detective eyes. "It was a volcanic island. It's been flooded and engulfed by the sea, about a hundred years ago. It isn't on any map, and radar doesn't pick it up anywhere."

"Wow."

"Wow is right. These people all died at the same time, and somehow ended up under your house." Grunt strokes his beard. "It's been quite the challenge finding information about this place. Which makes me wonder, Miss Stacks, how in heaven's name you heard about it."

Grunt is a serious looking detective, as serious as a guy behind a stainless steel table in a police station needs to look, and normally I'd be afraid of going down for all this, even though I didn't do anything other than not report the shit that happened in my dreams, of all places. But his underlying jolly Saint Nick vibe keeps me cool.

"I seriously don't remember. Oh, I think it might have been in a magazine?"

"National Geographic?" he asks.

"I don't remember. How did you learn about it, Mr. Grunt, if it's not on any map?"

"Detective Sergeant Grunt. And if I told you, Miss Stacks, I'd have to kill you."

I snort.

He leans towards Wolf. "What about you, mute boy?"

"I've never heard of the place before, Sir." Wolf clears his throat. He sits stiffly in his chair, the Santa aura not soothing him like it does me.

Grunt frowns and continues, "I hear this is your second fire this year, Miss Stacks."

"That's correct."

"Not very lucky, are you? Well, I wish you better luck getting back on your feet. You know what they say: third time's a charm. Or is that: good things come in threes? That can't be it. Fires aren't good."

"Bad luck comes in threes?" I suggest.

"Yes, exactly. Be careful." He shakes my hand, and then, nodding to Wolf, "Mister Law, you keep her out of trouble."

"Uh." Wolf looks at me, as if asking permission to answer Grunt's request.

"I'm a big girl," I tell Grunt. "Oh, have your men found any cats?"

"Cats? Oh, I think there were a few snooping around, but they ran off. I'm sorry."

With a nod, he exits, leaving the door open behind him.

Heading out of the station feels like getting away with robbery, even though my pockets are empty.

"I'm sorry we burnt down your house," Wolf says as we walk down the street. "You had some nice stuff in there. And man, those new records. What a shame."

"The sound system was pretty sweet. But that's all shit that can be bought. All my keepsakes burnt in my first fire. Hey, do you mind if we go check out what's left of the house?"

"Sure."

A huge pile of black rubbish, random pieces of wall sticking out higher here and there, some remnants lying around with more distinguishable features than the rest of their charred buddies. Fridge. Bath tub. Television. That's all that's left of my rich-lady home. There are no cats.

I step over the yellow tape and walk right through the rubble, across to the back yard. Tweed rope is strung from post to post, delineating areas that are being excavated. The pool is busted into a gazillion slabs, one area of it cleared and dug out. The shed still stands. When I look inside, there are still a few garbage bags tucked away at the back.

"Shit." I ask Wolf to wait while I sneak in and open one of the bags. It's full of styrofoam pellets. "They're gone!"

"The bags?"

"The teeth in the bags."

"Well, sounds like they found them anyway."

Something stirs in the bush. I half expect it to be James. But out comes a white kitty. An extremely clean kitty, considering it escaped a fire and has been roughing it outside since. Then another white kitty comes out. And a brown one. And a calico one. Soon I am surrounded by dozens of kittens, rubbing up my legs with their purring bodies.

"Heeeey guys. You guys made it out! You're so clever. How ever did you get stranded up in those trees to begin with? You're much too smart for that."

I pet a few, and soon they all make their way under my hands to get their share, brushing against my palms, one after the other, in an organic current of fur. Wolf bends down and adds his hands to the mix. They all stop at once and stare at him. Pulling his hands back, he looks to me with fright in his eyes. Is he going to become cat food? But the critters, having quickly come to a collective decision, spread their trajectory to encompass his caresses as well. Soon we are both encircled in rubs.

"You wanna go?" I ask him.

"Sure. What about these guys?"

"They come."

"I don't know that my place is big enough."

"We get another place."

"Together?"

I hear the question, but I don't answer. It's too blunt, too big, too soon. But that was what I meant.

We take the back alleys so as to not attract too much attention with all our kittens, the walk taking a solid hour. We don't talk much on our way. The morning city noises are calming, and the whole trek to Wolf's den a much needed hiatus from the rest of the choking chaos.

# TWENTY

When all the kittens have found a nook to hide in or a ledge to lounge on, we each take a spot on the couch. Relief and exhaustion wash over me successively.

"I wish I could go back."

"To where?"

"To my regular life, with records, plants, uneventful sleep cycles, and dreams I forget in the morning."

"And the coffee shop?"

"Ugh. Except for that."

"You still hate people?"

I think about that for a minute.

"Kind of. I mean, I know people are just looking out for themselves. That's why they act like such shit heads; they're trying to get the most out of everything, and that unfortunately includes other people. They're just looking out for number one. But I understand now that it's out of fear that they do it. They fear being alone, being unloved, misunderstood, judged. So they say: 'Fuck it, I'm just going to look out for myself, and then I'll be fine no matter what. I'm not going to let the world hurt me.' Though they might not even realize they are thinking it, the result is they become inconsiderate bastards."

"And, how do you know this?"

"Because that's me. I'm a shit head, looking out for number one."

"You're afraid of being alone?"

"No. I don't know. Maybe? I feel quite confused, Wolf. Disoriented. As if I woke from a nap in the middle of the afternoon, and I don't know the day or the time. That's how I feel all the time lately. Dazed. Just feeling my way in the dark."

"Are you sure you're not dreaming now?"

My stomach pulls into a knot. I close my eyes.

Oh god, just this time, let it be real.

It's all crashing down on me. The ground is treacherous, tremorous. My toes are dipping right over the edge. I'm going to lose it.

I slowly open my eyes. I look at Wolf, look at the clock, look at my hands. I can hardly register what I see. The emotion of the last few days comes tumbling down and spills out in a deluge of soundless tears.

"I can't see. I can't see how many fingers." I wipe my eyes over and over with the back of my hands, and hold them out again, trying to count. Wolf wraps his arms around me. My breathing slows, and I relax.

"I have all my fingers," he says. "Count yours, now."

I do. Ten fingers. Everything is in place. The clock on the counter shows 5:30 in bright red, crisp and clear. I try to poke my finger through my hand, but it's as solid as it should be. I sigh, nod, and rest my body against Wolf's.

"I don't want to fall asleep," I mumble.

"Hmm. That's not going to be sustainable. You know that."

I sit up. "Why the fuck is this happening to me? Who are those Luumore people and how the hell did they creep into my life and die under my house?"

"Good grief, Edie. I have no idea. How did you find their supplements in the first place?"

"An ad in a magazine that had been left on my counter at the shop."

"Do you know who left it?"

"No, but would that make a difference? If these are fucking magical people, couldn't they slip an ad into any old magazine?"

"Maybe. Maybe not." Wolf shrugs and pets the kitty on the couch's arm. It purrs and contorts itself under his hand.

The day I found that magazine, I had hardly slept all night thanks to Eveleen and Shaah-rl. It seems so long ago already. I remember making a damn half-allongé-americano-with-caramel bullshit drink with my eyes half-closed. I remember being angry. Jack. Jack Ass was the last customer I had served.

"Jack Ass," I blurt out to Wolf.

"I'm sorry?"

"Jack Ass. He's the last customer I served before seeing the ad in the magazine. Maybe it was his. But, maybe not. It could have been left by a customer before him, and I just didn't notice."

Wolf stands up and goes to the kitchen.

"Real endearing names you got for your customers," he says over his shoulder as he fills the kettle with tap water.

"I did my best."

"Did you have one for me?"

"No."

"Oh." He turns the burner dial on max, pets a cat that's sitting on the counter, and comes back. "Do you want to know what I think?"

"Shoot."

"I think you should try to find this Jack guy. He's the only lead you have."

"Ugh. I kinda hated him."

"I kinda got that."

"I served him for years. He was the rudest customer of them all. He never looked me in the face. Not once! He would never speak to me, not even a hello."

"Well, then, he's our guy."

"What? Why?"

"Because he sounds like a total freak. Who wouldn't want to speak to such a beautiful lady?" Wolf sits back down beside me and threads his fingers in my hair, pulling me closer.

I want to tell him to fuck off, because that's my natural reflex. I know it's unfair, and dishonest to how I feel. So I kiss him instead. My pulse shifts a few gears.

"Whoa." Wolf pushes down the hands that are trying to undress him. "Don't you want to go and catch your guy?"

"I've got my guy."

I avoid his smiling eyes, and those of the fifty cats watching us make out.

The kettle whistles loudly and we ignore it for as long as we can.

"I got it," I say, pulling myself up. I look at the clock and I'm glad to see the numbers are still nice and crisp. It's 6:00 p.m. Another hour or so before sunset, and I'm dreading falling asleep, fearing that I might wake up to dream after dream. What if I were to stay stuck in there forever? Or what if I were to wake up, but thought I was still dreaming, and never trusted things to be real again? Ever? It's a terrifying thought. The coffee made, I bring the cups back to the couch where Wolf sits shirtless.

"Here you go, hot stuff."

"Ah, a nickname."

"Fair and square."

We drink in silence. It seems Wolf is respecting my weird need to not talk about our *relationship*. It pains me to even think of the word. Yet there's nothing about this that feels wrong anymore. Not that it ever really did.

"So how do we find him?" I ask.

"You don't know his real name?"

"Nope."

"He was a regular?"

"Yup."

"Well, maybe he still is."

"The coffee shop is already closed. I'd have to wait until morning. Fuck."

"What's wrong?"

"I really don't want to sleep."

Wolf chuckles. "Well, we have lots of coffee. And I know other things we can do."

I put my cup down, watching the reflection of the ceiling light sway in the syrupy blackness. "I'm serious, Wolf."

"So am I." He smiles, a playful spark in his eyes, and slides his hands up my back, unclasping my bra. My nerves loosen. Mindful of our bandages and soreness, my fingers curl around his arms and draw him closer, inviting him to lay me down.

The cats, who have now earned the title of peeping toms, perch all around us: on the floor, on the shelves, on the window ledges, on the table, observing us, as strangely as only cats can, their eyes locked onto our every move and motion, right up until dawn splits the horizon.

When the darkness dissipates, they pad up and crowd the window to watch the sunrise, and I do my best to stay awake, lying comfortably in Wolf's arms and wondering if I'd rather just stay here and never move again.

The reserves of coffee well drained, we trot out to the Café L'Aimé, hand in hand. It scares the crap out of me but I go along with it. He wants to hold my hand? Fuck it. It won't kill me.

We catch May just as she opens the shop. I suddenly remember Wolf and her having a fling and I stop in my tracks, breaking our chainlink. He swivels to fully face me, turning his back to May who stands in the threshold of the coffee shop.

"What's up?" he asks.

"Sorry, I just remembered … you two." I put the tips of my index fingers together and twist them back and forth, like we used to do in grade school to tease kids we suspected of having kissed.

"Ah." He shoves his hands in his jean pockets. "Don't worry. It never got far enough, physically or emotionally, for you to need to worry about it. We merely *grazed* each other on the path of coffee and music."

A pang of jealousy grows in my gut—my lower gut, lower than my butterflies, lower than my anxiety, just buried deep in the folds of my intestines with all the crap. That's right. Jealousy is shit, and it'll turn you into a monster if you don't kill it before it takes over the gut it grows in.

May's little head peeks over Wolf's shoulder from afar, looking at us with her innocent, round eyes, stupidly cute freckles and wild, red hair. I push Wolf gently aside and take a large stride towards her.

"Hello, May!"

"Hi." She smiles, her eyes skipping over to Wolf and back to me, sensing the alpha vibe I was projecting.

"So how's it been going?" I ask, making myself big and imposing. She looks at Wolf again, fidgets some, and leads us into the shop.

"It's been all right, thanks."

"Customers treating you well?" I know the answer to that.

"Yes, they're wonderful. I feel lucky."

Clearly she's gotten a whole batch of new customers and the old ones have all moved on, or died. I ask anyway.

"Could you tell me if a certain regular still comes around? He's kind of short, dark eyes, full head of grey hair. Tends to talk on his phone and ignore you. Or me. He ignored me, all the time. He tipped big though."

"Oh, I think I know who you're talking about. Ya, that's, um ... his name is Ray."

"He speaks to you?" I'm feeling outranked, outplayed, betrayed.

"Of course. He didn't speak to you? How strange. You're so ... approachable." She pinches her lips, holding back a smile. She's mocking me, the vile little pixie.

"Well, then." I walk around the shop, looking at the ugly decorations that have been hanging for years and haven't gotten any better looking with distance. Wolf takes over where I left off, his voice too soft for my liking.

"We kind of need to find him. Do you mind if we, well if Edie, hangs out until he passes? I need to open the shop."

May looks at me like I am some stinky stray. Why the sudden dislike for me? I got her the job, the boy. Ah, the boy. I got the boy. She's jealous of *me*. Well, then.

"Why don't you just go to where he works, instead? Up Lavender Boulevard, the cleaners, right beside the titty bar. I don't know what it's called. I just know it's beside the titty bar because he tells me about the girls that come out of there. A lot of them are customers of his."

We both stare at her. She shrugs.

"Apparently they get dirty."

"May has grown some claws, you think?" I ask when Wolf and I regroup outside. Wolf ignores my comment, distracted by his shop across the street.

"I have to work, Edie. Can you handle this alone?"

"Ugh, I don't know. He's like my arch-nemesis."

"Yes, but you're Edie, goddess of the dreamworld and the wakened shore, who can mess with your shit with a wink and a snore."

"Nice."

"You got this. I'd give you my cell phone, but it burnt in this crazy house fire."

"Convenient."

After observing me for a few moments, seeking a sign on my face that assures him that I'll be ok, he places his hands on my hips and leans in for a kiss. I kiss him back, more passionately than normally I ever would in public, and the shit-monster in my gut hopes sweet, approachable May is watching.

# TWENTY-ONE

The walk to Lavender Boulevard is only fifteen minutes. On the way, mundane thoughts drift through my head, reminding me to get my credentials remade, my bank card, a new cell phone, everything. I've been in a cloud and my responsibilities are meaningless. Everything seems fickle, surreal. Until my belly grumbles.

"Ray's Clean as a Whistle Dry Cleaner" printed in black letters across a light pink awning confirms I'm at the right place. There's a sandwich joint across the street. I use the pocket money Wolf gave me to buy a sub. I eat slowly, reluctant to confront him.

What if this Ray is the one who left the magazine? Then what? Suddenly the plan seems pointless and I'm just about to call it off when I see him exit his building and walk straight towards me. The bells above the door do a little ding-a-ling as he enters the sandwich shop. I hide behind my hand and take a large bite out of my sub.

"Good morning, Ray," the employee says.

"Good morning to you, Genevieve."

Ray's voice is deep. Too deep for his small size. And why is he so damn cheery and polite?

"The regular?"

"Yes, please."

*Please??*

I hear the clink of coins in her tip jar. He walks over to the window counter where I am sitting and nudges his butt onto a stool, which is just a bit high for him, right beside me. He pulls out a magazine and flips through the pages. Meanwhile I am chewing as if my life depends on it, focussed and, hopefully, invisible. But I can't help it—I lift the flap my fingers make at my temple, my elbow firmly planted on the counter, and peek at him.

"Here you go, Ray," Genevieve calls out. He stands up, and I relax a bit, thinking I've succeeded in not being noticed. He leaves to the same soft, jingling fanfare he entered to and scuffles back to his building. The magazine he was perusing is still beside me, and the page is open to an advertisement written in bright, bubblegum pink.

It reads: "Want to stay awake? All natural waking pill, made from the exotic plant Witwit, from the Pacific island of Luumore. No side effects other than bright and sharp thinking. No sleeping required."

"What. The fuck," I say out loud.

Someone sitting alone at a table looks up.

"I'm sorry," I tell him. "My life is officially unhinged."

He smiles and continues eating, shaking his head. I muster the nerve to get up on my feet. The magazine lies open beside me. I snarl at it before rolling it up and tucking it into my back pocket.

"Here we go."

My fist goes up to rap on the door, but I drop it. No need to announce my arrival. He's probably expecting me anyway. It seems this little rude man knows a lot more about me than I do about him. He knows it was me at the sandwich place. Unless he drops his psychic magazines beside any which person, targeting their problems to a tee. It could happen. He could be that magical. I'd much rather believe that, than to think Jack Ass has been *onto me* since who knows how long.

The door swings open easily. Ray stands behind a waist-high counter. And behind him, rows of plastic-covered garments hang on long metal rods. He smiles like he doesn't know me.

"Cut the crap," I tell him. I grab the magazine from my back pocket and wave it around like an accusing finger. "What the hell is this?"

"A magazine, Miss Edie," he says in that deep voice I would never associate with his face.

"Ha! So you *do* recognize me."

"How could I not? You've served me every day, for many years now."

"That's right, I have. And why have you never, ever spoken to me before? Huh? Huh?"

"It was important that I didn't."

"*Cut the crap*, I said. Why does your stupid magazine know exactly what's wrong with me? Did you make those pink pills?"

"I did."

"Holy shit." I didn't expect him to confess so easily. "Why?"

Ray scratches his head of grey hair, then pulls at his cheeks. He closes his eyes.

"What the hell are you doing?"

"It is time to tell you everything," he says, letting go of his face and placing his hands on the counter in front of him. He looks uncomfortable, like he has an itchy tag scratching the back of his neck.

"Your cats," he begins, "they're here to test you. They're from … another planet."

"You're from another planet," I say.

"The pink sleeping pills you have taken were made with the extract of a very important plant from my island. Coincidentally, the cats have a similar plant on their planet. They had reserves, in the form of candy, but they ate them all on their way here. They need more to drive their spaceship home."

Ray steps closer to the counter and wipes his hands across its surface as if he was smoothening out folds.

"The plant has a component that acts in a special way with their blood. Just like you, Edie, but different. If they can eat enough at once, it should give them the boost they need to travel through the many galaxies that separate our worlds."

"I'm hearing you but my brain is only registering batshit-crazy talk."

"Listen, Miss Edie. This is very important. This plant extract has now multiplied in your bloodstream, which is why you don't need to take more to keep lucid dreaming. You are still lucid dreaming, are you not?"

I nod.

"You are now the living connection to my island. It is lost below the sea, as you may or may not know, and we need you to find it."

"You're from Luumore?"

"Yes, Miss Edie."

"All this time, in the coffee shop, you were one of them? One of those dead villagers under my house?"

"Yes. Though I'm not dead. I'm just old."

"All this time, you were trying to find a way to get me to take your goddamn pills? I don't believe you."

"It is the truth."

His truth makes me angry.

"Why do you talk to May?"

"May doesn't matter. So I talk to her."

"You're on some other level of fucked up, Mister."

"I didn't want to risk blowing my cover by speaking with you. And being impolite kept a necessary distance between us. I needed to wait for you to be ready. Now that you are, we can be friends."

"Fuck you."

"Where are the cats now?"

"At home. I mean, at Wolf's."

"Is Mister Wolf with them?"

"No, he's at work."

"They're alone? *Stuck inside?*"

"Yeah. What's the big deal? They're cats."

"You must get back to them, quickly! They will multiply! It's a stress reflex, Miss Edie. Either they overeat, like they did with the candy, or they copulate. They hate being trapped. They're escaped Kirnoons, Miss Edie—the tribe on the losing side of the century-long war on the planet Jubjub."

I laugh. "This is utter baloney. The other tribe, do they look like dogs?"

"As a matter of fact ..."

"Ok, I've heard enough crap in these last five minutes to balance out all your years of silence. Buh-bye."

"Wait! Miss Edie, you don't understand."

"What? What do I not understand? How crazy you are? You want to give me *more* proof?"

"You hold the key now, Miss Edie, in your blood. There's nothing you can do about it. You must keep dreaming, and change the landscape of the world until my island is brought back to the surface and the plant harvested."

"Why don't you do it yourself, hot shot?"

"I've tried, and failed. And there are no more of the reserves, Edie. I need the plant to do what you do. The last of the Tewtew is in you. And because you are … *special*, you don't need to take any more of it to dream-sculpt."

"Dream-sculpt." I chortle. "Ya well, I'm not more *special* than anyone else. Seriously! Why did you have to mess with my life! It was just the perfect level of messed up. Now it's off the charts."

"Edie, we're running out of time. You are ready."

"Ready for what?"

"To serve your purpose. To sacrifice yourself."

I want to punch him in the face.

"I'm out of here."

"The time is up, Miss Edie!" he hurries to say before I make it out the door. "You must help us or they will kill us all!"

I stop. "You're insane!"

"They really will, Miss Edie. They don't want to stay here, but they *will* take over if they have to. For now they know you are their only hope to get home and free the others who are still enslaved. So they will assist you as best they can. But if you refuse to help, I'm afraid you will be the first to go."

My arms dangle like weights by my side, the magazine slipping from my fingers and falling to the floor. Ray looks down at it.

"I apologize. The waking pill was just bait. It grew on my island too but is no more powerful than your green tea. You will have to sleep, Miss Edie. You must."

I consider the possibility of death by cats. It's easy enough to picture myself as James, my flesh being torn from the bone.

"You must go now, Miss Edie! The cats!"

"Ok! Ok! Geez!" I swing the door wide and take off in a jog, which turns into a run. I run down the street, until I pass Jane's plant shop, old crusty Frank, my burnt down apartment building, the Spin Factory. Hands on my knees, I retch from the exertion. Once in, I look around, heaving. The store is empty.

"Wolf!" I yell. He pops out from the back.

"Edie, what the hell happened?"

"Wolf, the cats. I gotta go open the door. Aliens. They're aliens. The dreams, they were on purpose. Ray.

He's from the dead people island. He says they're gonna kill me if I don't help. I gotta go."

"You're making no sense but I'm coming with you."

The store locked, we sprint into a run. I can hardly lift my feet anymore, the lack of sleep catching up with me. But a bad feeling keeps me going. I fear another fire.

We turn the corner and I almost want to cry in relief when I see that there are no red trucks, no large clouds of smoke billowing up into the sky. We barge through the door and stand in the middle of a perfectly calm and clean living room, the cats relaxing like well-behaved alien citizens.

"What a jerk!" I drop onto the couch. "He lied!"

"The place looks intact," Wolf says, looking around behind the couch, under the table, in the broom closet.

Petting a cat on the couch's arm, I start calming down, but then jerk my hand away. Could these cats really be out to get us? I stare at its furry little face. He's the cutest thing I've ever seen.

"Edie, come see this," Wolf calls out from the kitchen. There, nested between the counter and the opposite wall of cupboards and fridge, are fresh baby kittens. Dozens and dozens of hairless baby kittens. Normally I would gush, but there are so many, and they are so ugly, squirming on top of each other like wormy rats, that I scream instead.

A fat momma cat lies on her side, exposing hundreds of nipples. The newborns, still bereft of eyesight, shove their faces into her, clamping on and letting go, one after the other like a game of musical teats.

"He said they would take over if I take too long."

"The cats?"

"Yes. They're Jubjub cats." I shrink to the ground. Felines huddle around me. I don't have the heart to push them away. "He says I have to sleep. I have to sleep."

Wolf crouches down and reaches over the mound of fur between us to hold me. Silently crying in his arms, I feel the dreaded sleep crawl up my body, dragging a blanket of delicious numbness with it. It could be seconds before it reaches my head.

"Take me to bed?"

He picks me up in his arms and lays me down on his twin mattress, covering my legs with the bedsheet. By the time he pulls it to my shoulders, the other ghostly blanket has already enveloped me and taken me away.

# TWENTY-TWO

My eyes open to a black sky speckled with stars. I'm on my back, fully clothed, floating in my pool's cool water. Beside me is my rich-lady house as it was, before the fire and excavation.  I flip over and paddle to the edge. My sneakers are heavy below me. My jeans stick to my legs.

"Don't pee, don't pee," I say to myself, knowing that my sleeping body is warm in Wolf's bed and all this water might just entice me to relieve myself.

I check my hands. My fingers blur between five and seven on each. The fact that I know that I'm dreaming is surprisingly comforting. More so than being awake and not being sure that I actually am. In this ethereal moment, I am anchored. Time can't be trusted, the laws of nature don't apply, and it surely has its fickle moments, still, this world feels solid.

"Now what?" I try to remember what Ray said. The information feels faint and far. His island. I have to find his island. How would I do that?

The night is warm but I'm freezing in my wet clothes, so I strip down to my underwear and head inside in search of something dry to wear. On tippy-toes, I make my way to my room. The closet is full of someone else's clothes. That's fine. Weirder things have happened. I open a drawer and pull out a pair of jogging pants, then a T-shirt from another. I can't find any shoes other than high heels, so I go without.

Still being careful not to make any noise, I head back downstairs. The lights are off but I know my way around. I'm acting like a thief, and in my dream it makes sense, because this place doesn't feel like mine. It's not just the clothes, but the smell; the whole vibe of the place feels off.

"Elizabeth?" calls out a groggy lady voice. "Are you sleepwalking again, dear?"

"Shit," I whisper, and hurry out the door.

A switch is flicked on in the living room, and a yellow blanket of light gently drapes the yard. I'm hiding against the wall in a triangle of shade, and a few seconds later the world is dark again, darker than before, and I'm alone with the crickets.

Wolf and the cats come to mind, like an aftertaste, both bitter and sweet. My mouth is dry, my tongue motionless, in a body outside this one. If I rub my fingers against my thumbs, I can almost feel the bedsheets I'm lying on. The veil between worlds feels so thin, like I could slash it with my eyelashes. And though my lids are sealed with sleep over there, my eyes here are open. I realize more than ever that I can do anything. In this dimension, there are no limits.

So, how does one find a missing island in a dream?

Eyes shut, I picture the shore I played on once upon a time, the foamy water crashing around my ankles, the undertow pulling the sand away from beneath my feet. I see trees swaying in the wind, surfers carving the blue waves, and birds soaring above, waiting to catch sight of a meal below the surface. When I smell the salt, I open my eyes.

"Damn, I'm good."

An expanse of sea, blue as the sky above it, ripples calmly before me. It's daytime now, and the sand is hot from the baking sun. I switch from one bare foot to the other until I decide to step into the surf. I turn around and scan my surroundings.

A few people lounge in swimsuits under parasols. Others chase small, squealing children like they would scurrying mice, running in and out of the water, colourful buckets full of shells swinging in the grips of tiny hands. Further is a boardwalk, running along the edge of the beach, with shops set up along it. Beach bums and tourists meander out of their path to look at handmade baskets and jewelry, the need to be nowhere in particular apparent.

Kicking up the fresh water, my feet take me further down the sandy strip, until the beach bums are no bigger than my thumb. I strip back down to my underwear and leap into the water, diving as soon as it reaches my knees.

*This is a dream!* I remind myself with an inward yell, relying on this fact for my success, and my survival. The risk is huge but I'm not afraid. Death is not an option. This is *my* dreamworld.

Completely submerged, I avoid the undertow by staying low, near the seabed, paddling forward through the bubbles of my own escaping breath. Soon my body pulls and pushes for air. Giving in, I open my mouth and try to inhale. There's resistance, but finally the water breaks the barrier and rushes into my lungs. I brace myself for pain, for a burning sensation. Instead, it feels like light, warm pudding, and I'm glad I'm not suffocating.

There's a ledge before me, and beyond it a dark pool; a drop off. A knot tightens in my gut but I swim onwards, with the blackness of unfathomable depths beneath.

With the fear of being grabbed from below by something scary and unknown, something only the most sombre part of the imagination can conjure, my legs kick frantically, moving me forward nowhere near fast enough.

I squeak, attempting a most pitiful impression of a dolphin. Dolphins are friendly, and pull people around all the time. On TV they do anyway. The muffled sound drops almost immediately after leaving my mouth, probably because I don't know what I'm doing. I tread water, looking into the dark expanse, wondering where to go, and how to get there before I wake up. A light-coloured shape, a dot, appears afar. It must be the dolphin I so masterfully called. It's speeding towards me, rapidly growing in size.

"BOH SHHIIIT," I mouth in the water. It's a shark.

Its ugly face getting closer and closer, I start thrashing, but I know I can't out-swim the thing. Just as it's about to crash into me, it does a sharp ninety-degree turn, bumping me hard with its flank. The animal's teeth-like scales scrape the skin off my midriff, blood fanning into the water in a cloud of red ink. My hands catch its dorsal fin and hold on tight as my legs fly out from beneath me.

Heaving myself closer with my arms, I swing my legs around in a wide circle, over its head. I am straddling it, but facing the wrong fucking direction. His long body and tail start flapping from side to side, propelling us at an incredible speed. A stream of bubbles trails behind us, in front of me, mixed with blood from both my abdomen and the broken skin of my inner thighs as they rub against my sandpaper ride. I don't know where we're heading, so I send a thought into my subconscious, or wherever my intentions go in this land of the mind.

*Luumore.*

We zoom, at times close enough to the surface for the sun to infuse the waters and reveal the world of coral and fish, and at other times deep in the dark, where only trust in the beast I'm riding keeps my hands and bloody legs from letting go and waking up.

It is in such depths that the water suddenly becomes hot, like a bathtub. And it keeps getting hotter, almost boiling. I'm on the verge of screaming. An orange glow stains the blackness and I see it, flashing below us as we pass. The reason why I might now cook to death: a huge vein of bubbling red magma, so scorching it stays soft and fluid. A gaping mouth leading straight into hell's stomach.

Already it shrinks in the distance, the sudden coolness of the water feeling like ice to my skin.

"Waip!" I yell in bubbles to my shark, pounding its side with my fist. As I turn my head to see where it's heading, it crashes into a big wall of rock, knocking the consciousness right out of me.

I open my eyes. Wolf is beside me.

"I've got nothing," I say.

The cats gather around, the newborns already up and about, hairy and able. One meows like a grumpy old man, upset at my failure and clearly letting me know. The domino effect is instantaneous, and they all fall into ear-splitting laments, the decibels escalating, louder and more plaintive by the second. My hands slap to my ears, as do Wolf's. The glasses of water rattle against the coffee table and then burst, sending shards flying across the floor. We duck to avoid the shrapnel. Next to explode are the glass containers on the counter, and the glass-covered cupboards. One by one, they shatter with a loud crash. The cats keep wailing, like wolves howling to the moon, their volume deafening. The windows start to wobble.

"STOP!" I yell, as loud as I can, the alarm in my veins pushing my voice above the layers and layers of feline anguish.

And, surprisingly, they hush. If they had lips I'm sure they'd be pouting.

"For real, guys. Get a grip," I tell them. The blankets kicked off my legs and a few cats gently swept aside, I nudge myself to the edge. My inner thighs are burning, and my jeans are covered in blood. The sheets behind me are also soaked red.

"Fuck."

A few cats meow tentatively.

"I don't know what to tell you, cats! I don't speak meow." Aggravated, I drop my head into my hands, elbows on my knees. The quiet feels good.

Wolf rubs a few circles on my back and collects the bloody linen from the bed without speaking.

"Maybe we should give Ray a call." His voice resonates from the bathroom where he is shoving the bedsheets into his small washing machine. He returns with peroxide and bandages and a worried look on his face. The cats follow with their eyes as he sits beside me

"Why?" I ask.

"I bet Ray speaks cat. How else would he know all the stuff he told you." He addresses the cats next. "Does Ray speak cat?"

They all nod.

"There you go."

# TWENTY-THREE

"Well, obviously the cats understand English!" I say, trying to remember what we've been saying around them this whole time, and whether we incriminated ourselves in any way. I want to ask them about their evil plans.

I think up a list of yes and no questions. It keeps my mind off the teeth-clenching pain while Wolf helps me peel off my sticky jeans. He hands me a pair of shorts and calls the dry cleaner. Ray shows up before I'm done dressing my wounds.

It's strange to see his smiling face after years of hating his guts. But he's crawling his way into my good books. He brought doughnuts.

"Good afternoon!" he says, handing over the sweets. The skin of his neck is covered in little red marks. His arms too.

"Is that contagious?"

"What, those? No, not at all. I usually cover them, but no need to anymore. Um, do you have coffee?"

"Yes, Ray, but nothing fancy like you're used to," I tell him.

"Oh, I know what you're referring to. Yes, I had to contribute to your breakdown, push you right up to the edge, right? But it was all for the greater good. Regular coffee is perfectly fine." He takes a seat on the couch and welcomes a bunch of cats into his lap. "I see the Kirnoons have spawned. I warned you."

I sit on the couch beside him and pet my own slew of critters. Ray looks me over and frowns at my many bandages.

"I still don't understand why you picked me as your dreaming prey," I say.

"I didn't pick you, Miss Edie. They did." Ray smiles at the purring furballs rubbing up against his arms. He points to the box of doughnuts on the table. "Eat them while they're warm. The vanilla-strawberry ones are sinful."

"Look, Ray, I tried looking for the island. I really don't know how to find it."

"You need to *intend* it, Miss Edie, not *try to look for it.*"

"I did that! And it gave me nothing. Nothing except a good beating." A headache starts pounding at the memory, a bump on the side of my head proof of the crash. So that he might understand the shit I'm going through, I lift my shirt. My abdomen looks like I sled across a stretch of rocks, bright red where the skin has been scraped off. I have cuts and bruises everywhere. My inner thighs are as tender as raw sirloin, the blood of the wounds slowly soaking through the gauze.

"Look at me. I'm actually scared I might not make it back, you know? What if I die in there? What happens then?"

"I'm afraid that would be the end for you. This is what I meant by sacrificing yourself, Miss Edie. The cats have made sure you've been tested enough to be ready for this. To have nothing else to live for."

"What do you mean?"

"They've burnt down your houses, Edie."

"What?" I look at the cats on my lap and am just about throw them off. Instead I lay my head back and close my eyes, trapping some tired tears inside.

"They've been pushing you along, this way and that, so you'd get to a point where you wouldn't care for worldly things anymore, that you may understand the bigger picture."

"Which is?" I ask without raising my head.

"Sending them home. The bigger picture is them."

"A little self-centred are we?" I say in their general direction, which is everywhere.

"Vicious, but wonderful creatures." Ray nods.

Part of me wants to squeeze their little necks in my fists until they snap,  but I pet them just the same. It's hard to believe, though I know them well enough now to understand what they're capable of. They just want to go home. Who can blame them? The worst is, if they really are the perpetrators of my house fires, their plan worked. I don't give a shit about stuff anymore. Houseplants, turntables and records, TVs, east-facing windows. But I do care about life. Wolf's, Emily's. Mine. And at this point I'd do anything to have it all go back to normal. Whatever that is.

"Since it's so important to them, do you think the cats can help her find this island?" Wolf asks from the kitchen a few steps away. "You can talk to them, right?"

"Well, yes, I can." Ray squirms in his seat. "But they can't help her. It is she who must change the landscape." He turns back to me. "You must change the landscape, Miss Edie. With your mind."

The black-and-white tabby sitting on the ground, which I can no longer deny is my wild, jerky-loving street tabby, meows.

"I know that," Ray tells it. The cat meows a few more times.

"What did he say?" I ask.

"He says they aren't Oneiroi."

"What?"

"Dream gods. They don't have powers. They're not mystical beings or anything. They're just aliens that look like cats. I was an oneironaut; a dream explorer, like you. But you're a very special one, Miss Edie. Very different. Your mind mixes with the reality of things; you can shape it, and it shapes you in turn. The cats can't control anything in the dream world."

"But they've been in my dreams. And they did mess with things. They ate a guy!"

Ray suddenly appears uncomfortable, rubbing some red marks on his arm. He clears his throat.

"That is all very well, but they don't know where it is, Miss Edie. If they did, they wouldn't need you. None of this would be necessary."

"They could come into my dream and do their own thing. Look for it themselves. I'd give them *carte blanche* to my brain."

"Miss Edie, you need to understand. They cannot go into your dream and take the helm. It is your mind. You need to find the island with your own sheer intention."

Wolf sets a coffee in front of Ray, and one in front of me.

"And how is she supposed to do that?" Wolf asks.

"She shouldn't be drinking coffee, for starters," Ray points out.

I give him a disgusted grimace. That is the worst punishment imaginable.

"She needs to *intend* it," he says again.

"You said that already."

I pick up my coffee, smell it, and put it back down. "What about maps? Have you checked all the maps? Records? Navy records?"

"He wouldn't have access to those," Wolf says.

"But I do," Ray says to Wolf, "and I have checked. My island is gone. I was supervising it very closely, once upon a time, through my dreams. But it only took a minute, while I was distracted with a fried chicken sandwich and a red polka-dot skirt, for it to disappear. Gone. Like magic. I don't know where it went. But anything goes in dreamland, Miss Edie. It could be anywhere."

We eat the fresh doughnuts, breaking a few into tiny pieces for the cats to share. Ray stands and sees himself to the door, insisting that we stay put. Powdered sugar frames his large, sincere smile.

"Call me tomorrow. If I'm still alive. I've got horrible cholesterol. Good luck."

Just as he's about to leave the tabby meows again.

"Oh. Ok." Ray looks at me. "Volcanic rock."

"What about it?"

Ray looks back to the cat and up at me again.

"That's it. That's all he's got."

Ray leaves, and Wolf takes off for work not long after, promising he'll be back before nightfall.

"Wolf," I say, making him stall in the doorway. Approaching him with hardly any hesitation, I wrap my arms around his torso. He does the same to me, pulling me tight against him. I tuck my head into the crook of his neck, and I can feel him smile, even though I can't see his face.

With him gone, his bachelor apartment still feels crowded, the cats staring at me from all corners. In the bathroom I find everything I need to further attend to my wounds, and I resist drinking coffee though I almost break. I clean up all the broken glass and play fetch with the cats. Messing around on Wolf's computer, I google anything and everything that could help me with my stupid assignment.

Checking my bank account used to be a regular thing for me. When you don't have a lot, you have to pay close attention to your money. I suppose it's the same, or even more so, when you're rich, if you want to stay rich. I never had the chance to get the hang of it. Because my bank account is practically empty. It's surprising, and yet not. I know the exact dream during which it was drained. Leaving the forensic dentist with only a wad and a list in my pocket. That visit took all the money I had. That list cost me millions. I'm sort of sad, but mostly I don't care. The cats did their job well.

"Thirty years old and with the craziest life yet," I say to the little black cat that found its way under my hand. "If I find this island, you think I'll get my normal life back?"

A normal life with no fancy-lady house, nor a pile of money that was never really mine to begin with.

I look at little Blackie but realize all the cats are nodding.

"Wacky-ass cats. So, you guys are from outer space?" They don't respond. "So much for that." I throw one a piece of doughnut. He catches it with his clawed paws and brings it to his mouth.

"I thought you guys were super-intelligent or something."

They nod.

"So, outer space?"

A moment passes, and they nod again.

"And, you need me?"

Same response.

"Cool. And if I die?"

Nothing.

"Earth becomes your new home?"

They nod.

# TWENTY-FOUR

After an hour of pacing the small floor space, mulling over how to find this lump of rock, I decide to take a walk. Before leaving I remember that I don't have the keys, and most importantly, if I leave the cats alone they'll make another batch of themselves in their anxious preparations for taking over the world. So I stay put and flick on the small TV.

I find a black-and-white horror flick from the fifties. Villagers are running about in a panic, fast-moving lava at their heels. A volcano spits and drools, coughing clouds of smoke from its mouth.

*Volcanic rock.* I hear Ray's voice in my head. A quick search tells me there has never been a volcano nearby. *You must change the landscape, Miss Edie.*

And suddenly, alchemy. The idea crystallizes in my mind, and I'm much to excited to sleep.

"Guys," I address the cats, "can you help me fall asleep?"

Straightaway, all one hundred or so cats climb in and around the bed. I follow suit, squeezing into the fresh sheets under them, the jumble of furry bodies shifting around and piling on each other to accommodate me. They cuddle up, rub, tuck, and cat-massage my arms, my legs, my torso, and my forehead with their little paws, covering me completely, leaving only a small opening through which to breathe.

Then, they purr.

The bass-heavy buzzing overwhelms my senses, instantly sending my mind deeper into my body. I observe as if from afar: a thick layer of vibrating fat and muscle, resting lightly over long, splayed out bones. Bones that don't feel like mine. Blanketed with the calming roar of these man-eating kitties, I fall deeper, further and further away, until I cross the veil.

My feet are in the sand. The ocean, with its garnish of surfers, gulls, and small islands, is before me. Behind is the boardwalk, the huts and the strolling people. My dream replaying like a rerun, I'm already in my underwear. You'd think I would have intended a bathing suit.

I push my way into the waves, then dive in, swimming towards the drop off. The water rushes into my lungs more easily than the first time, almost as smooth as air itself. At the edge, already waiting for me, is a massive white shark. He is one ugly son-of-a-gun, massive scars etched all over his skin. I know he is there for me, so I wave like a twit and swim up to him. A light pat on the head reminds me of the shark's sandpaper skin. Reticent about getting my thighs cut up again, but not having intended chaps, I swing my leg over his back, hoping that this more calm and organized mounting will result in fewer injuries. But as I adjust my bottom, the blood puffs up, my skin already broken.

"I bbwant to go to the magma!" I bubble-yell out to the shark, who takes off as soon as he hears it. Dropping down low like one would on a galloping horse, I watch as best I can the dark sea-world flying past, my grip digging into his gills. The skin of my arms as cut up as that of my legs, blood is oozing from everywhere, and I wonder if the shark I'm riding might change his mind, skip the scenic drive and go straight to dinner. A quick check behind reveals a whole crowd of predatory fish emerging from the dark, each sporting rows of scalpel-sharp teeth and mean, beady eyes.

"Shhhit!" A stream of tiny bubbles sprays through my teeth. I kick my ride in the sides, releasing fresh blood from my legs. But my beast doesn't speed up. We travel upwards, towards the same corals we had passed last time, and I look behind us again. The light reveals a hundred-strong shiver of sharks gaining on us.

We are flanked on either side. Slapping my fish on its head, trying to get him to react, I soon realize that the new sharks show no interest in me, however bloody I may be. We are simply part of the herd. Jetting forward and down, we head back into the depths of the sea.

The water is warming up, a reddish glow ahead heralding the proximity of the crevice. The job will need to be done quickly, before I can pass out from the heat, before my skin turns into one big blister, before my eyelashes melt from my eyes. My imagination spiking in all directions, it would be smart to remember that dreamscapes respond well to intentions, whether good or bad.

We stop a dozen feet away, and I climb off, creating a fresh cloud of blood around me. I feel like an Oneroi of the Sea, with a cape of blood and an army at my side.

In the glow of the magma, I see my battalion clearly. Hundreds and hundreds of sharks, some on my side of the crevice and some on the other side, crowded in tight rows as far as I can see. If I don't move fast, these fish will either have me for lunch, or be cooked along with me.

I don't know how I had planned on making this happen on my own, but now with all these bodies waiting for my signal, I thank my subconscious, or whatever guiding hand responsible, for sending them along.

Gesturing with my hands from the ground upwards, I show the sharks I want the magma to come out. They aren't reacting, and I'm becoming dizzy from the heat. Obviously restless, they start wriggling harder.

I look around, eyes wide. "Shhhit!" I stomp, in a slow watery way. Once, twice, over and over. "Explode! Explode!" I yell.

This time, the sharks react. All hundreds of them start swimming away, upwards.

"Nooo!!" I yell. "Where are you going?"

Abandoned. I drop my arms, but quickly realize I've no time for self-pity. They're leaving. Too bad. I still have to cause an eruption. Put my energy to the ground. Make it vibrate hard enough. Make the island. I can do this. Time is running out. I might burn to death, I probably will. I'm probably going to die here. They'll find me dead in bed, boiled. That was the whole point, right? Push her until she doesn't care. Until nothing else matters. Until she is willing to sacrifice her measly life. I feel myself breaking down. My defences fall like armour plates, one by one. Thud. Thud. The will to fight is gone. It is all happening so fast. Facing the end. Time seems to stop. But I know there is urgency. It must be done. My own measly life might not be worth saving, but Wolf's life is. Emily's is. And all the other shits that live up there. I'll die for them. Not for me, and certainly not for the cats.

Fuck it. Death by cookery.

I put my hands to the warm sand, and concentrate. "QUAKE!"

Just as the words leave my mouth, the army of sharks come crashing down all around me, slamming hard into the seabed. The earth shakes.

Smashed to smithereens is another possible way to die today.

They swim back up some sixty feet, and speed back down again, like fat bullets. I paddle as fast as I can in the other direction. The sharks swerve moments before impact and slam their full weight into the ground, missing me by mere inches. They do it again. And again. The more they pound, the more the ground shakes, heat and debris rising. The crack starts to open wider. The magma bubbles violently. It's working.

A deep rumble from the belly of the earth rolls its way up, louder and louder. I swim harder. A gush of fiery red spurts from the sea floor, out into the open waters, cooking dozens of sharks on the way. Up and up it goes, quickly solidifying and oozing down its own sides simultaneously. A tail fin smacks me in the stomach, knocking the wind out of me as it launches me hundreds of feet away. It's my big motherfucker shark, and he just saved me from death by fire glazing. Crouched at a safe distance, I watch the growth of what I hope to be Ray's god-forsaken island, bathing in a billow of my own blood.

After what feels like an hour in dreamtime, the magma stops flowing, the lava solidifying into hard black rock. The water is slowly dropping in temperature. Like in my darkened room during a moonless night, my eyes adjust to the lack of light, but I see better than I should. The sharks disperse, but mine stays close, circling around me as if I am lunch. But I know I'm not.

I grab his dorsal fin and he zooms up to the surface. My brain should have exploded from the change of pressure, but it doesn't, and I'm grateful for the distorted laws of physics.

The sun is blinding and the air feels fresh in my lungs. I breathe it in, somehow without emptying out my warm, pudding water first. I'm almost afraid to see my reflection in case I've changed into a frog. It could happen.

Still growing steadily is the mass of black rock. It looks as though the sea level is dropping, exposing the formations underneath. Small waves crash around me, the waters disturbed by the island that is taking form. And then finally it stops.

My shark stops circling around me long enough for me to grab his fin one last time. He takes me to the edge of the rock, and leaves without saying goodbye. I know he's just a shark, but I feel like we've been through enough together that I'd have appreciated a small acknowledgement. A short stare-down. Some inkling of humanity. But we take what we can get.

The black rock is jagged and steep. My fingers curl over sharp ledges while my feet scramble for a stable surface to push up from. Without looking down, clutch after step after heave after haul, I lizard my way up. But I am slow, and the island of dreams is faster, it seems, than even its creator. Grass and plants come to life right under my hands, growing and poking out between my fingers before I even have time to move to a higher position. Blindly seeking the edges that are now covered in green, my bare feet slip easily, rocks scraping the skin off my knees as I dangle from my fingertips. By the time I make it to the top, everything hurts and everything bleeds. But the island is verdant and in full bloom.

At the edge of an overgrown wall of flowering grasses, I plunge my hands in and push the growth aside until I emerge in a open plain. At its centre, a crowd of tribespeople stand, apparently waiting for me.

"Hi." I give them a small wave of the hand.

The tribesmen wear leather wrap-around skirts, and nothing else. A few women stand amongst them, wearing the same skirt, their breasts bare. They have no jewellery, no weapons. Standing in my underwear, painted in drying blood, I feel that I meet the dress code.

"Luumore?"

A few of them nod.

"This is wonderful!" I smile, looking around. A full pivot shows me only grass and, beyond that, the sea and nothing more. We could be somewhere not far off the west coast, but I know better than to assume.

"Where are we?"

They shake their heads. In my dream logic, I know they understand me, even though they won't give me the information I want. I'm about to speak again when a sharp pain strikes in my upper jaw, right at the root of a tooth: the canine on the top right.

I put my finger to it. It wiggles under my touch and hurts, but in a satisfying way, like an over-scratched bug bite that still itches even though it bleeds. So I keep moving it, back and forth, the pain climbing up my face and into my eye, burning, titillating.

Unable to resist, I yank the tooth out. A tiny snap for a tiny tooth, pinched between my thumb and forefinger. It looks perfectly healthy, only it's too small, like a baby tooth.

My gums begin to throb angrily, swelling under my lip. The flesh quickly becomes engorged, pulsating with small, strong fists, punching the walls of skin holding them in. My face is going to burst, I think, as I cup my hands under my mouth, expecting an incredible mess of blood and bones.

Plop.

A second tooth falls into my hands, from the hole left by the previous one. Just time for a sigh, and another plops out. And another. Then, tooth after tooth, they stream through the empty hole like water from a tap. Shivers run up and down my body as it spews out its enamel gems, and I hold back my urge to retch. Only soft ticking resounds as the teeth land on top of each other, ending in a tall, precarious mound in my hands.

Lightheaded, I blink many times, breathing deeply to steady myself. The tribespeople shift their feet, necks craning to observe my new treasure.

Seeing their interest, I push my open hands towards them in an offering.

"Where are we?"

A man steps forward, a toothless smile pulling at his cheeks. Will he make himself a chomping tool with mine? I wonder. He cups his hands in front of my own. As I tip the teeth over, he speaks numbers and letters. I know I will forget by the time I wake up.

"Do you have a pen?"

He looks behind him and gives a nod. A woman, billows of fat falling over her leather skirt and breasts wider than her torso, approaches with small, dragging steps. A glowing, red-hot rod in her hand, she grins at me, mischievousness twinkling in her eyes and milk dripping from her nipples. She presses the fire-hot metal it into my skin and I scream myself awake.

# TWENTY-FIVE

The room is dark, night having fallen while I slept. Someone jerks to a sitting position on the couch, and another rushes to my side.

"Edie, it's ok. We're here." It's Wolf. He smells funny.

"You smell funny," I tell him.

"I think that's you."

I feel a sudden stinging pain in my forearm, and I recognize the smell of burning flesh.

"Son-of-a ... She branded me!" My tongue reaches up to my canine to see if there's a hole, but there's a tooth there, and I'm quite relieved. That would have been the end of my beguiling smile.

Ray stumbles up to me, excited. "You've done it, Edie. Those are the coordinates to the island." The cats meow softly in unison. "That's right, Kirnoons. You will be able to go home now."

Ray leaves to pack his bags while we wait with the cats, their eagerness apparent in their constant moving about. They hop up on the furniture, they hop down, pace, hop up again, making me dizzy.

After his help is refused, Wolf puts on a record and sits at the small table, his fingers drumming to the beat while I dress my new wounds. He seems ok with my stubborn autonomy. Though I'm not about to relinquish it, having him by my side has given me extra strength, no matter how much I profess my love of being alone.

"Thanks for sticking with me through all this stupid shit," I say.

"What are you talking about? My life has never been more exciting. It's fabulous. I'd do it over again in a heartbeat."

"Don't you find it scary? Disorientating? I feel like I've been on the verge of insanity since that first pill. I'm sure you feel a bit crazy too."

"I guess I do, a bit. The risk of you dying, while you attempt all this … That's the most scary part. But you aced it. I knew you would."

He smiles, and I wonder what will happen when all of this is over. Will I run away from him? Will I stick around for possible heartbreak? For once, instead of wanting to protect myself, I'm afraid of hurting another. Wolf doesn't deserve any anguish from me.

The cats stay behind. Leaving the back window open, as Ray suggests, allows them to come and go from the apartment. Easy contraception. Why I thought they needed to stay indoors I don't know. It seems I forgot that—other than getting stuck in trees—these first rate hustlers fare quite well out in the streets. Beef jerky is an impressive treat to score on a regular basis.

Ray, who doesn't stop surprising me, has his own helicopter parked in the large lot behind his shop. He settles into the pilot seat, with me beside him. Wolf, who didn't have to twist my arm much to get me to agree to his coming along, sits in the back. We buckle ourselves in and, at Ray's insistence, strap on some headsets with microphones.

The ground falls away, the lights of the city getting smaller and smaller. We head westbound in the dark blue sky, towards the Pacific.

"Ray!" I yell over the noise of the propellers.

"Yes?" he answers without yelling. I hear him perfectly in my headphones.

"How did you know I couldn't sleep when you first left me that magazine?"

He looks at me briefly before turning back to face the sky ahead. "I've been keeping a close eye on you, Miss Edie."

"You never looked at me!" I yell, though I know I don't need to.

"I have very acute senses, Miss Edie. I didn't need to look at you."

"You have superpowers?"

"No."

"I wouldn't hold it against you," I say now more quietly, looking ahead.

"I don't. I'd just been waiting for the opportune moment to slip you the pill."

"I knew you were really an asshole. No one is that good an actor."

"I knew you'd never trust me. You're not the trusting type."

"Well, what can I say. You trust people and then they break you. Or worse, they send you off to save the world at your own risk and peril."

"It was for the sake of the whole human race, Edie. You know, it wasn't long after my island disappeared that the cats found me."

Ray points to my arm with his finger and then with his chin. I flip it so he can see the numbers and letters seared into my skin. He then enters the latitude and longitude coordinates into the helicopter's GPS.

"Where were you when they found you?"

"Looking for a remedy on the mainland. We all used the plant to lucid dream, and it killed us all, in the end. All but me. Thanks to the Kirnoons. They have been keeping me alive for the last thirty years."

"What are you talking about? I thought you were dying from old age and bad eating habits."

"Yes, lately that has been my problem. But I am very old. I should have died a long time ago. The cats and I, we have a little trade going on. But now that they'll be leaving, I guess I will be too."

I feel no emotion about him dying. I still don't like Ray. It would take many more boxes of doughnuts, and proper conversation with lots of eye contact, for me to care.

"What kind of trade?"

"The cats like human flesh. So I let them suckle."

"That's disgusting! Those are the spots you have? They're kitty hickeys?"

"Of sorts. And, in exchange, they leave a small amount of venom. It boosts my system. Keeps me going. But sometimes it's not enough." Ray clears his throat, clearly hesitating.

"What's not enough?" I ask.

"Well, sometimes I have to find them people." He looks over to me and back to the front. "To eat."

I choke on my spit and it takes me a few moments to breathe properly.

"Geez, Ray! Can't they eat animals like the rest of the carnivores on this planet?"

"Apparently not. It doesn't taste like their native food. Humans do, though. And they took a liking to shrimp. Nothing tastes like shrimp where they're from."

He fiddles with some buttons, taps his thigh nervously.

"I told you the plant killed everyone from the island but me. Because you can't just use Tewtew forever without expecting some sort of repercussion."

It hits me that he's letting me know I will be getting sick, too.

"It's stuck in my blood forever," I say.

"I'm afraid it is."

"Why the fuck did you do this to me?"

"Please, Miss, your language."

"I think I've earned every right to express myself in any which way I want. This is a fucking outrage."

"The cats have concocted a remedy, but the cure is only temporary. You will still, eventually, die."

I look out the window. The world is pitch black. Nothing to see, nothing to distract me from the news of my mortality.

"Won't we all." I cross my arms tightly to contain my anger, my disappointment in life. I feel betrayed. "So, tell me, why did you drag me into this? Why didn't you *dream-sculpt* this damn island yourself?"

"I've told you before. My health is horrible. And yes, partly because I've been eating too much fried chicken, for much too long. But it's mainly because of the Tewtew. I couldn't take more if I wanted to. It would kill me. Really, I should already be dead. But the cats found me. I had opened my business cleaning garments, after years of dumpster diving and petty crime. I was still using then, and I would try to locate my disappeared island every night, in my sleep, to no avail. I was getting weak. The cats knew it when they found me. But they needed me then, the same way they need you now. So they kept me alive, and decided you would take over the effort."

"The cats decided?"

"Yes. They are most clever."

"But why me?"

"You have the right blood type. You were created in very special circumstances. Just in case."

"Created?"

"They were there when you were ... conceived."

"That's messed up." I remember the cats watching Wolf and I, on the couch, and shudder. Looking back on them, some things seem worse than they were at the time.

"Your mother and father were bestowed some of their venom while they made you."

"They suckled on my parents *while* they made me? I'm going to need therapy."

"Well, it's never too late."

"What's that supposed to mean?"

"I have watched you your whole life, Miss Edie. I know it hasn't been easy for you. Sometimes, it's best to talk about these things. Opening up can help us heal."

At that, I chuckle and look away, seeing nothing out the window but staring out nonetheless. There are too many memories I don't want to let in, and knowing that Ray is privy to them makes me shut down even more. If I have been doing ok at all these past years, it is mostly thanks to not digging up the past. I've left it all behind to die. How is it that this man is suddenly in my life, turning it inside out?

It all comes down to the damn cats.

"We've all been keeping an eye on you ever since you were born. The Kirnoons had a hand to play in most of your hardships," Ray says.

"I can't believe this."

"Like I said, they're vicious. Anyway, that is how I came to agree to help."

"Agree to help? I bet those crazy fuckers threatened to eat you up."

"They did. But still, I agreed to step in because I could tell you had very little will to live, and very little to lose. I thought it would be worthwhile to give purpose to your life. You were the most apathetic creature I ever met."

"Whoa! High and mighty a tad? You might have been spying on me through thick and thin, but you don't know what was in my heart. I *loved* my uneventful, hand-to-mouth life. I was in control. I was *free*. I prefer that life to no life, any day." I consider my impending death and feel a lump climbing up my throat. I quickly swallow it down.

"Well, you survived the task."

"Survived." I consider the word. I would like to think that I've done more than merely survive, but I know that the word all too accurately describes my life. My life that will be cut much shorter than I expected.

I look back at Wolf, who is quietly listening to our conversation. He smiles and winks, as if to uplift my spirits. But still, he looks sad. As if winking is his way of trying to hide it. I wonder again if I'll break his heart, and somehow I know it is already broken. Already was, this whole time. And I'm reminded: him, me, everyone. We all hurt. There's no escaping pain.

Ray turns and gives me a gentle smile, one that shows his years of struggle and diligence. It shows in the way his eyes crease, even if the corners of his mouth raise barely high enough to be admitted into the smile category. He looks relieved, like he can finally let go. And I hate him less. Because he, too, is only human. Albeit old and weird.

Flying in the dark, for all I know we are completely lost. I feel disconnected, without any roots, any home. Nothing familiar to fall into. It's unsettling.

"Do you miss your friends?" I ask Ray.

"Less now than I used to. I know I will see them soon."

"Were you able to visit them in the dreamworld?"

"I could not find them, Miss Edie. Nor could I find, or make, the island. You have succeeded so quickly. Most impressive."

"Well, I didn't have a choice, did I? The cats were already stress copulating. It felt like the beginning of the end."

Dawn finally tints the sky, stealthy slivers of light slipping over the edge of the earth. No one speaks, the silence only broken by Wolf's random humming, turned on and off like a radio with bad reception. About an hour after sunrise, I start worrying we're going to run out of gas.

"How are we on gas?"

"Don't you worry, Miss Edie. We are almost there."

As he says this, a black mass seems to appear out of nowhere; a mound of dirt and trees in the middle of the ocean where seconds ago there was nothing. Ray pushes on the stick between his legs and the helicopter tilts forward.

The smile on his face is now unmistakable.

He handles another lever and we start to lose elevation, his feet keeping us on course by means of pedals. In moments, we are hovering just above the ground, blowing the crap out of all the plants around us, and I imagine I'm in one of the movies I've seen where the plants get the crap blown out of them by helicopters. Ray cuts the engine and we jump out before the blades quit spinning.

Looking around, I recognize the same island as in my dream: the same vegetation, the same flowering grasses, the same open plain. But there is no one in sight.

"The islanders must still be asleep."

"I believe, Miss Edie, that we won't find anyone here. The villagers have been dead for a long while. I'm envious that you got to meet them."

It hadn't occurred to me I'd given my teeth to ghosts. I shudder to think of the fat branding lady, and wonder if Ray was related to her. Perhaps she was a second cousin, or an aunt.

We walk across the open area, into the tall trees that cover most of the island's surface. Past a jungle of lianas, branches and roots, we reach a smaller clearing than the first, this one covered with a low-growing bush.

"At last," Ray says as he plucks at one and lifts it to his nose, breathing in its scent. He then tucks the leafy branch in a bag slung around his torso. "Don't pull out the whole plant. Snap the branches a few inches away from the stem."

We do as he says and spend most of the day harvesting Tewtew and tucking it into our own sacks until they can't take another twig.

"That's it for me," says Wolf. "My bag's full."

"Me too," I say.

Ray turns to us, leaves sticking out of the flaps of his bag, of his breast pocket and of his cargo pants side pockets. "I'm stuffed too." He reminds me of myself in a dream not that long ago, standing in front of a vomiting ATM machine, my clothing stuffed with bills. I point to the edge of the field where there are still a lot of harvestable plants.

"What about all of those?"

"We leave them. We have enough. And what we took will grow back."

"We should burn it," Wolf says.

"Oh, absolutely not!"

"Don't you think it's too much power for one person, or even a small tribe, to be able to mess with everyone's reality?" Wolf asks.

"There's no one here!" Ray says, looking away, pushing the herbs deeper into his pockets. "No one! Why bother with it? It bothers no one! Besides, only Miss Edie can shape life. We could only ever explore." He checks his breast pocket again and gives it rapid little taps.

Wolf and I look at each other, wondering why Ray cares so much about letting the crop survive. But the island is unpopulated, as he says, and so we shrug and follow him back through the jungle and out to the helicopter. The sun has fallen from its perch by the time we climb back into the aircraft, and are once again flying in the dark.

An uncomfortable silence accompanies us home.

# TWENTY-SIX

"What are they saying?" I ask Ray once we arrive back at Wolf's flat to an excited choir of mews.

"They're very anxious to get home."

"And so how will they do that?"

"They have a spaceship, parked on a rooftop downtown."

"Of course they do."

"It crashed there, thirty years ago. They've had time to fix it since."

"Thirty years, huh," I look them over. The cats meow steadily, piddy-paddering all over the apartment. I'd be restless too, if I was about to return home after thirty years of being stuck on a planet run by hairless bipeds.

Though I'm happy they will be vacating the premises, part of me has gotten used to them being around. Then again, they are murderous, leaching vampires. They can go.

"What about the cure?" I remember.

A few cats meow aggressively.

"They've been working on a way to make it better," Ray says.

"Working?"

"Yes, um, they've been ironing out the kinks, telepathically. This big black-and-white one says that you were always generous with your jerky, but ever since you saved them from the trees, they've taken an even bigger liking to you. They hate being stuck in trees."

"Why the hell did they climb them, then?"

"The dogs dared them to. Cats can be so prideful."

"Wait, so she won't die?" asks Wolf.

"Of course she'll die. We all will. It's the when that no one knows. Her 'when' is just subject to more uncertainty."

I plop down on the couch, ready for a dreamless sleep.

"Will I stop lucid dreaming?"

Ray looks at the cats and then back at me. "Do you want it to stop?"

I consider it for a while. "I don't want to be confused. I don't want to *dream-sculpt* anything. The potential for fucking things up is too great. It's too much responsibility."

Wolf smiles. "I thought you liked being in control."

"Let's just say I would prefer some mystery to my future. That's the normal thing, right? I'd like normal right now, even if that means uncertainty." I avoid his eyes, just like I avoid the question gently flickering in them, a question I don't know the answer to myself. What about us?

The cats huddle into one large mass of fur in the centre of the apartment, taking up almost all of the floor space of Wolf's tiny bachelor apartment. The black-and-white tabby pads forward and hacks out a huge fur ball, spitting it out at my feet. I hesitate, because it's disgusting, but I pick it up and turn it around in my fingers anyway. It's wet and gooey and oddly heavy. A few cats meow.

"Inside the furball," Ray says.

"What?"

"Look inside."

Prying my fingers deep into the ball, I tear the goopy strands open and find a small, hard centre. A pink pill.

"Aw man, not this again."

"This will give you extra time, Miss Edie. But it will also end the lucid dreaming."

I put the pill and the blob of hair on the coffee table.

"Thanks, guys," I say to the cats, but also to Ray and Wolf.


The bags of Tewtew are dumped on the floor and the cats jump it, gobbling it all up and stuffing themselves to the point that they look like they are each expecting a full litter of kittens. Ray fidgets like a junkie jonesing for a fix. Once done feasting, the cats sit and stare at me with the roundest of eyes. My own gaze wanders to the two other humans in the room, pleading for a clue as to why I'm under sudden scrutiny. Maybe they are about to attack. But they stay put, staring, until their eyes begin to glow a bright red.

"Space cats!" Wolf hollers in laughter.

They all turn to look at him and he freezes immediately. The big tabby cat, which by now we know is the leader, emits a series of sounds: garbles and clicks and soft screeches like an old fax machine; nothing that sounds like a cat.

"They're leaving now," Ray says. As he says this, the hundred felines come and rub themselves against my legs.

"Ok, ok. You're welcome, crazy kitties. I'm glad you decided to let me live." I pet as many as I can. They turn to leave, and one little black cat comes running back and jumps up into my lap. He purrs and lets out a little squeak.

"This one wants to stay with you," Ray says.

"Really? Oh. Well, as long as he doesn't try to kill me."

Ray looks at the tabby. The tabby looks at the black kitten. All three nod.

"Ok then, welcome to the family." Wolf twitches and I realize what I've said, regretting it instantly. I focus on the kitten. "I'm happy to have you stay, little one."

Ray clears his throat. "I'm leaving too."

"Oh, yes. I'm exhausted too. We should all get some rest."

"No, I mean I'm leaving town. I'm dying anyway, probably in a few weeks. I'm going to fly back to my island and end my days there."

"That's why you didn't want to burn the crops. To use one last time," Wolf says. He walks over to Ray and gives him a hearty handshake, rattling his small frame. "Have a good trip, Ray. The biggest adventure yet."

"Yes, er, indeed. Miss Edie." He nods at me. I get up and give him a hug. He's a long way from the Jack Ass I once knew.

Ray leaves first. The cats face me in serried lines; a regiment of furry faces. Their tails all spike up straight in unison, as if in salute. So I salute them back, as does Wolf.

"We'll miss you, crazy cats," I tell them. I'm not sure it's the truth but it seems like the right thing to say. We watch them leave out the back window one by one. "Well, that was the weirdest thing to happen to anyone, ever."

I flop back down on the couch, exhausted. I look at the clock, a habit that I have lost in the last few days. The hands both point to twelve. The apartment is bright with noonday sun, but all I want is to delve into slumber. I remember the pill. Before I can ask, Wolf hands me a glass of water.

"I support whatever decision you take," he says, "but obviously I'd rather you don't die just yet. Sounds like some restful dreaming might be a good thing right now, too."

Nodding, my mind trails off. I turn the pink pill in my fingers. I haven't explored space, yet. Or trained in any martial art. It's been mere minutes since the cats left, the glow of their eyes almost still lingering behind, caught on the thin film of time and space. How quickly we can forget. I toss the pill to the back of my throat.

"Thanks, Wolf."

"I know."

I put my legs up on the couch. Wolf climbs onto his own bed and leans on his elbow, looking at me from across the small space. My mind wanders to the near future, and I remember that I have no money left in the bank.

"Am I poor again, Wolf?"

"I don't know. Are you?"

"I don't have any money left."

"Apparently."

"Yet, I don't think I'll ever be poor again."

"You're rich, Edie."

"I am."

I flip onto my side and close my eyes.

"If you had money," Wolf continues, "what would you want to do with it now?"

A few moments pass.

"I'd want my own nursery," I answer, my eyes still closed, "and a bigger apartment."

"With me?"

Another moment passes.

"Ya."

I fall into a deep, dark sleep and stay there all day and night, finally waking completely refreshed with the golden dawn sun gushing in through the window. I don't remember my dreams, and I don't mind one bit. I know we always dream, even if we don't recall them upon waking, but it feels good to imagine that my brain had at least one night's respite.

That day, Wolf heads out to work to get things sorted out and back on track, and I decide to call the Cedar Residence. I wouldn't mind chatting up George and Jim, if they're still alive. If they aren't, I'll play cards with whoever needs the company.

First, I ring up Emily.

"Hello?"

"Hey Em."

"Oh, hi."

"I hope you're not too angry with me. I kind of got caught up in some crazy animal rights activism. It just took over my life. But I'm back now, and I'd like to ... Well, I'd like to be part of your life. And for you to be part of mine."

There's silence at the other end of the line.

"Em?"

"Yes, of course. I'd love that."

I can hear her smile.

In the news: a meteorite shot down from the sky, landing in the middle of the Pacific and obliterating a small, previously undetected, volcanic island.

Frank, old as dirt, is still on the streets giving his regular crap to passersby.

Jane still runs her shop, and agrees to give me some tips, and even have me supply some of her plants once the nursery is established.

James is alive, miraculously, though badly scarred by what they say was self-mutilation during extreme night terrors. He was promptly put on medication. He married a woman twice his age, and they bought a house in the suburbs which they are slowly filling with a fresh collection of salt-and-pepper shakers.

May decided to go back to school earlier than planned when Todd closed the café. The space is now a cobbler shop run by a guy named Wayde.

The Spin Factory is doing so well that the neighbouring building is being rented to expand the store. The back coat closet is still oftentimes used for entertainment purposes.

Wolf, Kitty Coal, and I move into the two thousand square foot loft upstairs. To celebrate, we buy our own espresso machine.

# ACKNOWLEDGEMENTS

I wonder if people really read the acknowledgments. Hi mom. As you may know, writing a book is a long process, an obsessive one, and a scary one. But I have found so much support around me. In my family, in my close friends, and in the Bookstagram community. I am amazed over and over again at how kind hearted the people around me are. Thank goodness because I'm a fucking fragile flower.

My husband Mitch, you beautiful man. I dedicate this crazy book to you. I think of the life we've built and how damn supportive you are, and my heart wants to implode in my chest. I love you. Thanks for accepting my marriage proposal and tarnished skateboard-bearing ring as we smoked cigarettes out on the porch that long ago day. Thanks for laughing at my bad jokes, encouraging my crazy ideas with way too much enthusiasm, and dancing in the living room with me. Long live the pointed-finger move. Thanks for saying "just keep making art", and doing all you can to make it possible for me. I couldn't ask for a better life, even with all the storms. Because the rainbows are glorious. I remember our early "dates", when we'd take walks downtown, window shop, and dine. Our conversations were always about our dreams and how we'd make them happen. And look, they have, and they are. There are no pills for these ones. And I promise, no cats :)

Special thanks to Johnna LaFaith, Steffi Brooks, Geneviève Rouleau, Pierre Tremblay, Verna Lindstrom, Lien Tremblay, and Tuesday Rain, for reading this in its early stages and giving me feedback. Thanks to Fred Gagné for helping me with proper police procedure.

Lastly, huge thanks to Sylvain Neuvel (author of *The Themis Files*, *The Test*, and *A HISTORY OF WHAT COMES NEXT*) for reading this book and gracing my cover with a blurb even though you were busy with a million other things in addition to travelling the world (and back again thanks to the pandemic.) Also, thank you for giving me a local hero to look up to.

## ABOUT THIS BOOK

In an attempt to trigger lucid dreaming and have a better grasp on what I was writing about, I *tried* to follow a regimen which involved going to bed earlier, drinking less caffeine (oh the suffering!), the regular counting of my fingers & looking at the numbers or the hands of clocks, the attentive flicking on & off of any light switch I came across, and the periodic, ever-dramatic, self-investigating question: "Am I dreaming?" I also regularly tested my solidity by trying to push a finger through my palm. I would wake myself up after a number of hours of sleep to log my dreams, chill a bit, and zonk back out.

To get to the point: I did not succeed. Not one lucid dream came of this short lived test. It was overall quite exhausting, and I was happy to just go to bed and sleep when I quit. But what *was* fantastic was waking up in the morning to some crazy mind explosions I'd written down, sometimes more gibberish than anything. These laughs alone were worth the effort.

About 95% of the dreams in this book come from those mid-night wakings. Some of the dreams I had years ago and still remember, also thanks to having written them down. And others I made up, but there was little need for that. Dreams are wildly fascinating. This here is some of the best fun I've had writing. I hope you had fun reading it.

# ABOUT THE AUTHOR

My name is Rachel(le) Tremblay and I'm a writer, painter, and musician from Montreal, Canada. I grew up speaking Frenglish, drawing on the floor as I dangled upside down from chairs and mimicking the songs my parents practiced with their band on my little kiddie organ. I'm generally an optimist, and I'm never bored. I believe days should be twice as long, with an obligatory nap sandwiched in there somewhere.

Other Books by Rachel Tremblay

Crash Kitty - An Off My Feet Origins Story (adult)
The Nirvana Threads (NA / adult)
Topaz: The Truth Portal & The Color Mayhem (all ages)

www.rachel-tremblay.com

About thirty years before OFF MY FEET. Five women share an apartment and Friday nights. Wine and creativity keep them well entertained and always on the brink of trouble. One doomful evening, an alien craft lands onto their building and brings mystifyingly charming creatures into their lives. Creatures they would never have suspected were sinister...

Boy, were they wrong!

Read the tragicomedy that started it all!

Turn the page to read the first chapter of the novella

**CRASH KITTY**

**an Off My Feet origins story**

# Bloody Beach Sugar Sex Magic

"This is a dumb idea," Maddy said, her hand stretched out over the crystal bowl that sat in the centre of the coffee table.

"What if one of us has a disease, yet to be discovered?"

That was Lo, the hypochondriac. It was surprising she was going through with it at all. Even now, her hand quivered above the bowl.

Sitting on the edge of one of the two couches was Bee, whose job was to puncture the fingertips with a triple-disinfected needle.

But the idea was Kat's, and she told everyone to suck it up.

"Besides, I love you all so much, I'm ready to share any of your weirdo germs." Kat took a swig from her beer and slid up closer to Bee, kissing her on the cheek. She offered her hand, palm upwards, and grinned.

*"Ow!"*

"You want to bleed? Well, it's not going to tickle," said Bee, proceeding to make a dimple in her own fingertip. The skin pierced with a soft *pop*, a bubble of blood blossoming on the surface. "Okay girls, this is it."

Arms extended, the four young women looked at each other, a nervous energy passing from one gaze to the next. They were just messing around, they all knew that, but there was an eerie vibe to their little ceremony, a seriousness that transcended the bonds of school, work, and childhood. This ritual would make them family.

Lights dimmed, candles glowing orange among the bottles and glasses of leftover wine placed like chess pieces around the crimson-streaked bowl—it was perfect.

John Mayer crooned from the sound system, the volume low enough that he might actually have been locked in the broom closet, serenading them full-heartedly, desperately trying to push his charm through the door.

"What do we do now?" asked Lo in a whisper, her eyes saucer-round.

"We stick our fingers together where they were pricked so that we come into contact with each other's blood. It's dumb," repeated Maddy.

"It's *poetic*," corrected Kat, shooting a sideways glance at Maddy. "This way, whatever happens, we'll always have part of each other within us."

The others nodded, their smiles fading as they remembered Claire, who had died the year before after being struck by a mango truck.

"Fuck mangoes," said Bee quietly.

"Fuck mangoes!" they responded in unison, and pushed their fingertips together in a bloody kiss. Lo started crying, and that was that.

"Oh, baby," said Kat, crawling over to the couch opposite and wrapping her arms around Lo's shoulders. The other two blew out the candles and flicked on the lights, then sank back with their drinks, the thrill over and done with.

"Let John out of the closet, will ya?" Maddy said to Bee, who had the remote beside her. She cranked it until his luscious whining overpowered Lo's weeping. The girls sang along, Lo finally joining in for the chorus, her beer bottle now a microphone.

The song ended and Bee turned the volume back down. "Back in the closet you go."

"You know, I don't know why he has to make that face when he plays his guitar," said Maddy.

Bee laughed. "Come on, Maddy, he plays like a god. He's blowing his *own* mind."

"Or holding his guitar a little too snug," said Kat, pointing to her crotch, her eyebrows popping up and down. "He's really *feeling* it."

Giggles chimed likes bells in the small living room, bouncing against the bottles, the framed Led Zeppelin and Cream posters, the glass patio doors.

"I find it makes him less credible," continued Maddy. "Like he needs to convince us that he's really that good."

Kat came back to her spot on the couch beside Bee. "But he *is* good. So it doesn't matter—we're convinced either way."

"Are we, though?"

"I think Kat's right," said Bee. "He's *turned on* as hell. That is clearly his sex face."

They all howled.

"Fuck it, let him back out, poor bastard," said Kat. They turned the music back up and danced in the dining area (which had no table and was reserved for such shenanigans), playing air guitar and making sex faces as they sang along.

Bee bobbed over to the kitchen to make herself a drink.

"Make me one?" came Kat's slurred voice from behind. "Your bloody sunshine on the beach."

Bee turned and, seeing Kat's crooked smile, rolled her eyes. "That's not what it's called. And no."

"Why not?"

"You'll throw up."

"No, I won't."

"I'll make it virgin."

"It'll take a lot more than your crazy made-up drink to make me a virgin." Kat hopped her butt onto the counter, only to slip immediately back off and flop to the ground. The loud thud drew Maddy and Lo to the scene, who, upon seeing Kat sprawled out on the kitchen floor, burst into laughter so violent they shook like bags of hot, popping corn.

Kat was pulled to her feet and all four stumbled back to the living room, murmuring giggles and exulted sighs.

"I dare you to drink that down in one shot!" said Kat, nodding at Bee's drink.

"What are we, in high school?" Maddy shook her head.

Bee held up her glass to Kat and, after surveying her crowd with a dignified frown, downed it—but slowly, because the thing tasted good.

"Bloody beach sugar sex magic!" she gasped, wiping her mouth with the back of her hand. "I'm going to be rich. All right, then. My turn."

"Your turn for what?" said Kat.

Bee held a finger to her lips, then pointed it to Lo. "I dare you, Lo, to throw your bra out the window."

Lo tsk-ed. "We live so dangerously."

"We take candy from strangers!" Kat threw her arms up.

Lo reached behind her back, fiddled with the clasp, tugged here and there, and pulled a pink lace bra out through her shirt sleeve. The others followed her to the balcony, giggling.

The apartment was six stories high, the building's last, and the people below were far enough that they looked small, but not so small that you couldn't throw a rock at them if you wanted to. It was eleven, and Friday nightlife was bustling.

"You need to toss it out far if you want it to land on someone," instructed Maddy.

Lo bent over the railing, Kat and Bee holding her by the waist in case she toppled. Dangling from her fingertips, the flimsy piece of cloth swung back and forth as she tried to give it momentum. Finally, she swung and, with a grunt, hurled it into the night, her upper body tipping forward with it. Fingernails dug into her skin as the girls held onto her, though they couldn't help following the bra down with their eyes. Being lace, it had no weight to it, and caught in the wind before whipping back towards the building, landing on a balcony a few stories below. A head popped out, and then a hand clutching the pink bra victoriously. The girls hooted and hollered, to which the guy holding the bra looked up and smiled.

"Hi!" he called.

The girls laughed, waved, and retreated.

"Oh, you guys, you clawed me good," said Lo, rubbing her flanks. "I'll need some alcohol for that."

Maddy passed her a bottle of Jack Daniel's.

"Not that kind, you jerk." Lo laughed her way to the bathroom and came back with some rubbing alcohol and cotton swabs. "Okay, my turn. Maddy."

"Yes?"

"You're going to call Jack."

Maddy pointed to her bottle of liquor quizzically, raising an eyebrow.

"No," said Lo slowly. "Work Jack. You're going to confess your love for him."

"Shit, we *are* back in high school. Look, this is the only Jack I need in my life."

"Ya, right," said Kat. "You won't shut up about him. *Jack's got great hands, Jack's so funny, I want to climb up a tree with Jack and bone.* Anyway, you have to take the dare, Maddy. It's the rules."

Maddy threw up her arms, the whiskey bottle flailing. "What rules? I didn't agree to this."

"The blood thing," said Bee. "We did the blood thing. Now, you take the dare."

"You guys suck." Maddy took a swig of her preferred Jack and then reached for the cordless phone on the end table. She dialled and waited. It rang once, twice, three times. Her smile grew as the rings continued.

"He's not there," she told the girls, her smile by now a wide, smug grin.

*"Maddy?"*

"Oh, crap." Maddy almost dropped the phone. "Err, yes, hi Jack. It's Madeleine. I have to warn you, I'm drunk, and I'll fully regret this on Monday morning, if I remember any of it. If I don't remember, please play along and forget I ever said anything."

"Okay?"

"I ... you ...."

The girls snickered.

"Shut up! Damn it." She turned back to the phone. "Anyway, Jack, you're, well—you're one heck of a guy."

The girls laughed even louder. *"One heck of a guy!"* Kat howled.

"Come on, guys! Pipe down!"

"What's going on over there? Are you having a party?" asked Jack.

"Not really. It's just the girls and me."

"The girls?"

"Ya. Look, I have a stupid crush on you, that's all I'm going to say. This is dumb. Bye." She hung up, cheeks throbbing pink.

"Damn, that's going to hurt in the morning!" said Kat, wheezing with delight.

Maddy, still blushing, muttered something into her whiskey bottle. Kat poured another glass of wine.

Bee, still choking back giggles, stood and headed for the kitchen. She re-emerged with another homemade drink for herself and a beer for Lo. "It's your turn, Maddy," she said.

Maddy looked up. "Who's left?"

"Me," said Kat.

"Ha! Kat, you little fox. You wanna play schoolyard games, I'm throwing it to you old school. I dare you to kiss"—Maddy looked at the girls—"Bee. *With* the tongue."

Lo squealed. Bee and Kat, side by side on the couch, looked at one another.

"I give you my permission," said Bee, turning to face Kat and closing her eyes. Kat licked her lips, swallowed hard, and inched closer.

"Do you all have to watch?" she asked.

"Of course!" said Maddy. "That's the whole point, isn't it? It's just a kiss. Don't be a baby."

"I guess, but this is Bee."

Bee waited, eyes still closed. "Come on, Kat." She puckered up. Kat slipped her hands behind Bee's neck and pushed her lips against Bee's. They both opened their mouths in obedience to the dare, their tongues dancing—uncomfortably at first, but the heat rose quickly and they held each other tighter, the kiss deep and long.

"Whoaaaa," said Lo and Maddy, both mesmerized. Bee finally pulled away, panting.

"Damn alcohol," said Kat, shaking her head. She straightened her clothes, seeking composure by means of a deep breath. Bee said nothing, her cheeks flushed and her gaze dropping to the bottles on the table.

"John, where are you?" Kat called suddenly, an edge of irritation to her voice. She reached for the remote, stretching over Bee's lap, who watched her closely. The volume pumped up and the girls relaxed into the song.

"Gosh, he's so yummy," said Maddy.

"Hey, you can't have them all, Maddy. You have Jack, leave us John," said Kat.

"The sex faces, though," said Lo.

"All right, all right," said Maddy, who was trying very hard to look sober, straightening herself up and putting on sophisticated airs. "We played dare. But that's a child's game. How about something a little more risky?"

Lo frowned. "What's riskier than dare?"

"Truth." She smiled.

www.ingramcontent.com/pod-product-compliance
Lightning Source LLC
Chambersburg PA
CBHW030243120726
47903CB00005B/1592